Remember to EAT and Other Stories

Praise for Remember to Eat

"Luminous, thought-provoking stories centered on three generations of women carry me back to coming of age in Queens, New York, shining a light on the odd and often misunderstood expectations of changing times. Mazel tov to talented educator and award-winning author Meryl Ain. Remember to read *Remember to Eat*."

—Marilyn Simon Rothstein, author of *Who Loves You Best* and *Crazy to Leave You*

"Reading *Remember to Eat* is a bit like stepping into a time capsule and seeing the women who stood before us and, at times, stand alongside us. Ain skillfully illuminates the Jewish narrative—her characters come alive, and we as readers share the ride through their struggles and their triumphs. This is a great book club read, something every generation can appreciate!"

—Adina Genn, journalist and author

"Meryl Ain's wonderful new story collection, *Remember to Eat*, takes its mother-daughter characters through almost a century of American Jewish life. Compelling, poignant, and often funny, the stories are well worth reading!"

—Deborah Kalb, author of *Off to Join the Circus*

Remember to EAT and Other Stories

MERYL AIN

SparkPress

Published in 2026 by
SparkPress, an imprint of The Stable Book Group

32 Court Street, Suite 2109
Brooklyn, NY 11201
https://shewritespress.com
Library of Congress Control Number: 2025915437
ISBN: 978-1-68463-340-1
eISBN: 978-1-68463-341-8

Interior Designer: Andrea Reider

Printed in the United States

This book is dedicated in living and loving memory
to my mother,
Helen T. Fischman,
who showed me that storytelling is an act of love
with its power to enlighten and enrich our lives
from generation to generation.

Table of Contents

1

Remember to Eat

Marjorie became pregnant on the first try only a few months after she and Eric married. A few months later, the doctor confirmed that she was having twins. This was a total shock to both Marjorie and Eric, since there were no twins in either family.

As a physician himself, Eric wanted to be a partner to his wife in the pregnancy and birth process. But as Marjorie began to look as if she were carrying an elephant, developing sciatica, swollen feet, varicose veins, and an overall sense of malaise, she kept reminding him that it was not *they* who were pregnant, but she.

It was daunting to order a layette for two and to cram two cribs into their small apartment as her due date approached. Marjorie often thought to herself that if she had known how quickly she would conceive, she might have waited until they bought a house.

As uncomfortable as she was, she was in no hurry to give birth. The thought of pushing out two babies frightened her, and she secretly hoped for a cesarean section. She had absolutely no idea how she was going to care for two infants at once, especially after hearing her grandmother say to her mother, "Our baby is having babies." She was twenty-three and scared to death.

But Eric was having a field day. The hospital where he worked as an orthopedic surgeon offered Lamaze classes, and if a couple attended the program, the husband would be a partner—a coach to his wife during the birth process. Toward the end of the pregnancy, the couple attended classes together, which Eric took very seriously. Meanwhile, Marjorie kept hoping for a cesarean.

It was the hottest August on record in nearly fifty years, so other than attending Lamaze classes, Marjorie stayed on the red paisley couch in their air-conditioned apartment, watching TV, eating ice cream, and reading pregnancy books, which included all the unlikely complications that might occur.

About three weeks before her due date, on her second Carvel sundae, lying on the sofa, watching *McMillan & Wife* with Rock Hudson and Susan Saint James, she got up to go to the bathroom and felt a warm gush of water. She called Eric, who was at the hospital, and being no ob-gyn, he said: "Oh, it's probably pressure on your bladder, but you better call the doctor."

"Have you had a contraction?" the doctor asked.

"No, not yet."

"Your water just broke and you're in labor. When your contractions are ten minutes apart, come to the hospital."

She quickly called Eric back to let him know that he should stick to his own specialty and come home right away.

"Oh, I haven't had dinner yet. Have you?"

"No, but the doctor told me I can't eat. Just hurry home in case I start getting contractions."

Although the hospital was only ten minutes from their apartment, it took Eric close to an hour to return. While Marjorie waited for Eric to come home, she had her first contraction. She was starting to get angry—what could be taking him so long? Was it another patient issue or did he not understand the gravity of the situation? Just as her first contraction ended, Eric walked in with a bag from Katz's Deli.

Marjorie groaned as she saw what he had bought himself for dinner: not a corned beef or turkey sandwich, which would have been quick and understandable, but a southern fried chicken dinner with french fries, coleslaw, green beans, and a knish on the side. For dessert, there was a very large piece of gooey chocolate babka.

"You might be in labor all night," he said by way of explanation when Marjorie gave him a look. "Don't you remember how they told us in Lamaze class that the husbands should remember to eat?"

"That's what you got out of the class?" Marjorie asked incredulously.

"No, not just that."

About six hours later, the contractions became more intense, stronger and more regular. At ten minutes apart, Marjorie grabbed her go-bag and the couple headed to the garage to get their car.

As they pulled into a parking space in the hospital parking lot, Marjorie began to get a contraction. Before she realized what had happened, Eric had taken off, leaving her alone in the car. Here she was, married to a doctor, in labor, sitting alone in the car. By the time he returned ten minutes later, she was in tears.

"Where the hell did you go?" she yelled.

"I went to get a wheelchair for you."

Her mother always told her that Eric meant well, Marjorie reminded herself. She supposed he did, but he was not the world's best communicator.

Once Marjorie was admitted and on the floor, the doctors announced that the labor was progressing nicely. They hooked her up to a machine, which registered the intensity of the contractions.

Eric focused on the machine. Each time his wife moaned and groaned, he remarked on the force of the contraction. But each time he said, "That one wasn't so bad," she wanted to smack him.

Instead, she cried out to anyone who would listen: "When can I have an epidural? I need one now."

After about the fifth time, the nurse replied. "It's too late, honey."

"What about a cesarean?"

"Oh, you don't want that or need it. Before you know it, this will be over, and you won't even remember the pain."

Adam was born at 5:47 a.m., weighing 6 pounds, 6 ounces, and at 5:58, Seth weighed in at 7 pounds, 1/2 ounce.

When the twins were about two and a half, Marjorie became pregnant again. She and Eric had always wanted three children, and they decided there was no point in waiting. Marjorie had repressed the panic and chaos of the twins' infancy and was of the opinion that she deserved a medal for having survived it, especially with a husband who often put his patients before his family. This new baby was going to be a singleton and it would be a pleasurable—and much less harried—experience, she believed. She had survived, and so had the boys, and now she was the repository of wisdom and experience on babies, judging from the questions her pregnant and new-mother friends asked her.

One sunny April day Marjorie found herself with nothing for the boys to do. Her neighbor Dara had said she would invite them to her daughter Lacey's birthday party but later told Marjorie that she had changed her mind and decided to make it an all-girls event. Marjorie understood but was a little miffed, especially because now she had to occupy the boys herself.

She took them to lunch at Friendly's and they both had their usual grilled cheese and french fries. They were good eaters and, thankfully, behaved in restaurants. They ate their lunch and scribbled on the activity sheet. After lunch, Marjorie thought she would take them for a short errand, and then she would bring them home and put them down for their afternoon naps.

She strapped them each into their car seats in the back seat of her brown Plymouth and headed to Midway Department Store, where they had the kind of pregnancy bras she needed.

She took the double stroller out of the trunk, unbuckled the boys, and strapped them into the stroller. But they were getting older and didn't like to be tightly harnessed. They squirmed and fought her. Marjorie didn't think there was any danger of their falling out of the carriage, so she let them stay unstrapped.

She quickly found the bra counter and began to contemplate which one she should buy. Minutes later, when she looked back at the stroller, both boys were gone. She panicked.

"Adam! Seth!" she called. "You can stop hiding now. Where are you?"

There was no answer and she started frantically going through the racks of nightgowns and robes near the bras, thinking they were hiding there. She began to panic more when she didn't see them. She started running around the store, sweeping the clothes aside on each rack, calling their names. She screamed to anyone within earshot: "I've lost my sons; please help me!"

Where the hell are they? she thought as she began to sob. The worst possible scenarios jumped in her head. Maybe a child molester had snatched them? Perhaps they had been kidnapped? Were they being poisoned or brutalized at this very moment that she stood by helplessly? What kind of negligent mother was she anyway?

"I can't find my twin sons," she breathlessly told the older woman at the counter.

"Oh, they must be hiding," said the employee. "I've got a couple of sons, and they keep me on my toes. Come with me, we'll tell the manager."

Marjorie followed.

"Maybe they went to your car," the manager said. "What does it look like?"

"It's a brown Plymouth, but there's no way they found their way to the car, and anyway it was locked. They're toddlers." Marjorie was frustrated with the ignorance of the manager.

"I see," said the manager. "Describe to me what they look like and what they're wearing."

Soon the manager announced on the loudspeaker, "*We're missing two little boys who are two and a half years old. They're identical twins with brown hair and brown eyes, and both wearing blue shirts and black sweatpants. Please come to the front desk if you find them.*"

Marjorie was paralyzed. Normally she would call her mother or Eric, but she was too ashamed. In her mind, she beat herself up. She didn't deserve to have children. What if she lost these two? They would surely take this unborn one away from her. Eric would scream at her, but, she hoped, her mother would sob and hug her. But maybe she would yell at Marjorie too. How could she go on living after this?

How could this have possibly happened? People even told her she was a paranoid mother! She had averted her eyes for only a few minutes. She thought again of predators and kidnappers and child molesters; the world was a dangerous place. *What an idiot I am! What a horrible person! How could I go on living if I've lost my precious sons?*

After two more announcements—while Marjorie frantically checked each aisle again and again—the manager told her he was almost sure they weren't in the store. "The security guard combed the place. Do you want me to call the police?"

"Yes," Marjorie sobbed.

The police were called, and while she continued going in and out of clothes racks she had already looked through a million times, Marjorie unraveled her life, thinking she had tried her best to be a good mother. She couldn't imagine going on living without these two, and who would care for the new baby when she ended up in prison or a mental institution? Eric would probably divorce her. Oh, how she wanted to call her mother, but she simply could not inflict this pain on her—not yet anyway, not until she knew how this was going to end.

It ended about twenty minutes later.

Between the shoe and lingerie departments, the manager approached her again, this time smiling. "They found them! They're bringing them back now!" He led her to the front of the store, then out the front doors, just as four police cars rode up.

A young, uniformed police officer with blond hair and blue eyes quickly got out of the car and approached them. "Are you the mother of the two missing boys?" he asked. "We've found them and they're in the police car."

"Thank God!" she screamed, as another cop escorted the two boys to their mother. She put her arms around both of them and sobbed as they hugged her back. Adam's face was tearstained and one tear rolled down Seth's cheek. Marjorie embraced them, whispering a prayer.

"Where were they?" Marjorie wanted to know.

"They got out of the back door to the store and walked to a fence, which had a hole in it, then climbed through the hole into the schoolyard. The children were at recess. The school nurse called us."

Although relieved, Marjorie was dumbfounded. "How did they get out? They're not strong enough to open an outside door like that."

"Someone must have held the door for them."

Marjorie was flabbergasted by this. *Was it really possible for someone to be so clueless as to hold a door for two unescorted little boys? What a moron. It must have been a man—he should be arrested.*

Marjorie thanked the police officers and continued to hug her sons. She kept thinking that if they had been gone for ten minutes, she would have yelled at them. But after ninety minues of anticipating the worst, she was just relieved they were alive and well.

"We rode in a police car," Adam said.

"But they didn't turn the siren on," Seth added.

Marjorie wasn't sure if they would remember this incident, but it impacted her forever. A couple of years later, the story of Adam Walsh made headlines. He was kidnapped from a Sears department store and murdered by his kidnapper.

As her children grew, the only time she truly relaxed was when they were sleeping upstairs in their beds.

2

Mother-in-Law

As she dressed for work, Marjorie sang the words to "Mother-in-Law," Ernie K-Doe's 1961 number-one hit. When she was a junior high school student, she thought the tune was catchy. Back then she had no idea what it meant. But now she wondered. Was she really a miserable person, who was intent on destroying her son and daughter-in-law's happiness? Now—more than forty years later—the words stung.

That's what her son Adam's soon-to-be wife, Cara, thought of her, she was sure. Despite all her efforts to keep her mouth shut and her pocketbook open, Marjorie had slipped up. It didn't matter that she and Eric were paying for half the wedding or giving them the down payment for their new home. She had even bought a beige dress for the wedding, as per Cara's instructions. And Marjorie was well aware that she did not look good in beige; she needed a little color to lighten up her face.

Her mother, Alice, who thought the sun rose and set with Marjorie, had even remarked when she first started dating that bright colors complemented her and that she should always remember to reapply her lipstick. But now, Marjorie had no choice but to go along with the program. Cara insisted on accompanying her to Dina's, her favorite dress shop, the one where she had bought her outfits for the boys' bar mitzvahs and Deborah's bat mitzvah. Those dresses had been blue and pink, red and purple, but Cara had been clear, and Marjorie would abide.

As soon as Adam and Cara got engaged, Marjorie began tapping the wisdom of friends whose sons had already married. She was determined not to make the mistakes her own mother-in-law had made. Once she became engaged to Eric, his mother, Ruth, had an opinion on virtually everything.

"You must use the band we used at Eric's bar mitzvah party. The bandleader played two trumpets at once and did a magnificent rendition of 'Romania, Romania.' And our synagogue is so much bigger than yours and the caterer knows us; we used him for Eric's bar mitzvah . . . You're making a mistake not getting a decorator. I'll put you in touch with Selma; she's redoing our den now. And you really should buy a house right away and not waste money on rent. There's a house for sale on our block."

Marjorie caved on the synagogue and the band, even though her parents were paying for the wedding. However, she refused to call Selma, and the newlyweds rented an apartment in another town.

In search of guidance, Marjorie invited two of her closest friends to her home for lunch. The three women sat at a round glass-top table in her kitchen, eating tuna fish and egg salad and drinking coffee.

"I'm not my mother-in-law, and I would never want to do to my children what she did to me, so please give me some advice," she said. "I know you have married sons."

"It's a lose-lose," said Pam. "At least you have a daughter. There's just something intrinsically competitive in the relationship—you both love the same man."

"Welcome to MOMS, the Mothers of Married Sons support group," said Linda.

"Is there really such a thing?" asked Marjorie.

"No, but there should be. Everyone has the same problem. No matter how hard you try, your daughter-in-law will resent you."

"But Diane said her daughter-in-law is like the daughter she never had."

"She's either lying or the ax has not yet fallen," said Linda.

Something was bothering Marjorie about the forthcoming wedding. Not the fact that she and Eric were paying half and had little or no say. She had been pleased that Adam had tapped his twin, Seth, to be his best man and his younger brother, Josh, would be an usher after walking Grandma Alice down the aisle. Adam's friends and Cara's married brother would be the other ushers, and Marjorie and Eric would escort their son down the aisle to the chuppah and stand under it with the bride's parents during the ceremony.

The day Marjorie accompanied Cara to Dina's for her bridal gown fitting, Cara mentioned in passing that she was having a wedding outfit made for her dog, Sadie, an apricot-colored cockapoo.

"The dog is coming to the wedding?" Marjorie blurted out.

"Of course," Cara said. "How could I possibly get married without my Sadie there? Wait till you see her outfit."

"They make wedding dresses for dogs?" Marjorie asked.

"Of course! It's gold fabric with a sequined design and a gauze hemline. And there's even a big flower on the front, which makes Sadie look even more adorable. It's made out of a high-quality polyester material that's soft and comfortable to wear. I don't want her to be uncomfortable."

"And is she going to sit with the guests during the ceremony? Where will she be?" Marjorie asked.

"Oh, no; she's going to walk down the aisle."

Marjorie's face fell. "She's going to walk down the aisle? Why?"

"Because she's my little girl. I couldn't get married without her."

Afterward, Marjorie agonized over whether she should have said something to Cara right then and there. This was the most patently ridiculous thing she had ever heard. Adding insult to injury, *Sadie* was her beloved late grandmother's name. But they were in a dress shop with other customers and salespeople. And Marjorie was in the habit of weighing her words, especially since she'd been warned by her friends. She muzzled herself not to speak in haste, especially in public.

But as she drove home, she got angrier and angrier. She realized what had been bothering her all along. Deborah, her youngest child and only daughter, was not in the bridal party, but Sadie would be playing a starring role.

By the time she reached her house, Marjorie could feel her heart racing. She took a glass of water, sat down at the kitchen table, and dialed her mother.

"That's insane," Alice said. "A dog walking down the aisle."

"I just assumed Deborah would be included," Marjorie said, "but now I'm thinking there's been no mention of what she should wear or anything."

"She probably just figured Deborah's a young teenager, so you can get her dress off the rack. It would have been nice of her to ask her to be a junior bridesmaid, though. Are you going to say something?"

"I have to, but I think I'll speak to Adam first. It could just be a misunderstanding, a mix-up."

Marjorie dialed Adam at work, and of course he didn't pick up the phone. He texted her back: "In a meeting; will call you back ASAP."

She wrote back: "It's important."

"I'm really upset, Adam," Marjorie blurted out when he finally called an hour later. "I've tried to not interfere and say anything about this wedding, but now I have to. Why would Cara want to hurt your sister by excluding her from the wedding party?"

"You know, I mentioned to Cara a while back that it would be nice to have her, and she just didn't think it was a good idea. She said she's too young; she wouldn't fit in with her girlfriends. She said she couldn't be part of the bachelorette party because it will be in Las Vegas. There will be drinking and gambling and she's only sixteen."

"And she can't be in the wedding procession without going to Las Vegas?"

"Well, you know Cara is a bit rigid. She likes things just so."

"Tell me that the dog is going to Las Vegas."

"No, of course not."

"Then why can't Deborah just walk down the aisle?"

"Well, I think it's also a matter of the shower. The maid of honor and the bridesmaids plan it and pay for it."

"Fine, I'll pay her share. Is Sadie contributing?"

"Oh, Ma, don't be sarcastic. What do you want me to do? I want Cara to be happy. It's her day. I don't want to spoil it for her."

"Who's in the bridal party besides the dog?"

"Her sister is the maid of honor, and her cousin and some friends are bridesmaids."

"How many are there in the party?"

"Six bridesmaids and the maid of honor."

"And the dog," Marjorie added, trying to contain the sarcasm she knew she was dripping. "And she can't include your baby sister? This is a forever thing, Adam. It's a wedding. There'll be photos. Everyone will notice that she's not in the procession. Don't you love your sister? Do you really want to hurt her this way?"

"Fine, I'll talk to her," Adam said.

Each day, Marjorie waited for Adam to call her, but it seemed he was in no rush.

This could not be a good sign, she thought.

Finally, on the eighth day, she called him.

"Did you talk to Cara? The wedding is a month away. What's taking so long? What did she say?"

"Mom, she likes to have things just so—the way she pictures them to be. She doesn't want a teenager in the bridal party. We've been fighting all week. She said you've spoiled everything for her."

"What doesn't she understand? This is family."

"I just don't know, Mom," he said as his voice cracked.

On one hand, Marjorie was sorry she had ever said a word. On the other hand, how could she not? This would not only put a blot on the wedding, but it would be cast in stone: in the video, in the wedding album, in Deborah's heart. It would impact her fragile self-esteem. She was so sensitive. Marjorie could not bear to see her child excluded. How dare Cara come into this family and drive a wedge between siblings? Marjorie was livid but held her tongue.

"So, what's the bottom line, Adam?"

"She'll do it, but she's not happy about it."

"Fine," said Marjorie. In another situation, she would have given both of them a lecture about how family is forever. But the damage was done. The wedding hadn't even taken place yet, and she had already become the hated, disruptive mother-in-law. Her son was marrying a spoiled brat. Who knew if the marriage would last? If so, would Cara drive a wedge between her and her son? Would she even let her see her future grandchildren?

"So is Cara going to invite your sister to walk down the aisle or are you?"

"You can do it, Ma."

The day of the wedding, everyone looked picture-perfect in their wedding attire. Of course, Sadie stole the show. Marjorie put on her widest smile as she and her husband escorted Adam down the aisle. Cognizant that the entire event was being videotaped, she kept reminding herself to look dynamic in her beige dress. She even forced herself to smile at Cara's mother in her royal-blue gown.

The entire family held hands and did the hora together during the reception—captured on video and in still photographs for posterity. During the dance, the bride motioned to Marjorie to join her in the middle of the circle. Together they danced, whirling round and round as the guests danced by, cheering and singing "Kol Chasson v'Kol Kallah," the traditional Hebrew song in honor of the bride and groom. Marjorie was determined to keep up with the bride yet felt herself getting flushed. She saw Adam with a big grin on his face fly by with the others. She was grasping at the moment, not wanting it to end. Finally, out of breath, she had to stop. Cara threw her arms around her and said, "I'm so happy to be part of your family."

Adam brought Marjorie a bottle of water and walked her to the table, just as she saw Cara lead Deborah into the middle of the circle, repeating the same dance routine with her, also culminating in a hug. She wondered, *Who is the real Cara—the bridezilla or the actual bride?* Maybe she would be more relaxed once the wedding was over. Didn't she come from a nice family? Time would tell.

"What a beautiful family! What a gorgeous couple! You are blessed!" The guests exclaimed as they hugged Marjorie and offered their mazel tovs.

Marjorie smiled graciously and thanked them for coming. But in the background, she kept hearing the words to "Mother-in-Law" over and over in her mind. It would be a very long time until she gave her opinion again.

3
Family Circle

Although the world was at war in December 1943 and a number of their cousins were enlisted in the armed forces, the Gildner Family Circle held its annual Hanukkah party as usual. Sadie had suggested to her daughter, Alice, that this would be the perfect time to introduce her fiancé, Albert, to the family. Both Alice and Albert were home on leave from the US Army, and there was now a brand-new diamond ring to show off.

That year, the party was in Aunt Clara's home in Brooklyn because she and her husband, Morris, had the biggest house with a private garage. The rooms were oversized, and as guests walked through the double-door entry, they were greeted by stained glass, gorgeous hardwood floors, a decorative fireplace, columns, and exquisite moldings.

When Sadie and her eleven siblings lost their parents, they pooled their resources and bought a family burial plot at Mount Hebron Cemetery in College Point, Queens. While the hum of traffic was unmistakable, their family's section in the cemetery was a verdant parklike garden and had ample room for not only their parents but their children and future grandchildren.

Uncle Morris—or Moishe, as his siblings called him—was the richest member of the family, having made his money in the jewelry business, and he helped finance the purchase. But to sustain it, the brothers and sisters formed the Gildner Family Circle with annual dues, monthly meetings, a Hanukkah party, and Passover Seder. As Moishe said, "We're burying our parents and keeping their memory alive at the same time."

After the potato latkes, cold cuts, and desserts were served and multiple menorahs lit, Aunt Sarah, who was the lone spinster of the clan, prided herself on distributing the Hanukkah gifts she'd bought for the children. These took the form of cheap plastic dreidels and toys and chocolate Hanukkah gelt. The little ones would line up and get their gifts from Aunt Sarah, and then Uncle Moishe would give each a brand-new shiny quarter. Then the children would run off to play in the basement, and the Family Circle meeting would begin in earnest.

Up until this point, Alice had been pleased with the family's reaction to her handsome fiancé. Dressed in uniform, he was six foot one with dark wavy hair and hazel eyes. Height had been a requirement for Alice, because at five foot seven, she didn't think most of the young eligible Jewish men were tall enough for her.

While she was in college, before joining the Women's Army Corps, Alice and her friends wrote letters to many young men in the service. They believed it was their patriotic duty. They wrote whenever they were asked, to their friends' brothers, cousins, sons, nephews. When Alice received

Al's first letter, she was impressed with his exceptional vocabulary but couldn't help but feel a little annoyed. He used the word *vesicant* and then, in parentheses, wrote "blistering." Although Alice didn't know the meaning of the word, she was insulted that he assumed she didn't know how to use a dictionary.

But that didn't deter Alice's friends. Immediately after reading his letter aloud, four of them offered to take his address and write to him if she wasn't interested. Observing the interest from her peers, she quickly changed her mind.

"If I don't like his next letter, I'll give his address to anybody who wants it," Alice announced to her friends.

However, instead of another letter, Alice received a phone call. Al was home on furlough and wanted to meet her. Knowing that some of her friends were also meeting their military pen pals, Alice agreed without hesitation.

Three days later, when she opened the front door to her parents' home, there stood a tall, good-looking young man in an army uniform. Their eyes met and he flashed a wide grin.

"Wow, you're a tall one," she said as she ushered him in. "How tall are you?"

"I'm six foot one," he said.

She invited him into the living room, and they both sat on the sofa. Within minutes, Alice's mother appeared with a big smile and cookies and tea on her best silver tray. She made a quick exit and Alice's father then entered. Al stood and they shook hands heartily.

After Alice's parents retreated to their room, the two young people sat in the living room and talked until midnight. For the first time in any young man's presence, Alice felt pretty.

When they parted that evening, he told her he was sorry he had waited until the end of his furlough to call, but that he would definitely write to her and hoped she would continue writing to him.

Alice graduated from NYU and days later enlisted in the US Army.

Just days before Hanukkah, less than six months after they first met, Albert gave Alice an engagement ring while both were on furlough. Alice had been stationed at Fort Belvoir in Virginia, where she was a reporter for the *Belvoir Castle*.

Alice, always concerned about her mother's reactions, could see that she was delighted that Albert was so well received at the Family Circle meeting. He was polite, good at small talk, and a college graduate.

Alice beamed as she signaled to Al how pleased she was with his reception. He blew her a kiss. After a meal of cold cuts and potato latkes, the lighting of the menorah, and the distribution of the gifts to the kids, the Gildner Family Circle was called to order. As always, the discussion started with the financing of additional graves for the family's cemetery plot. Then Aunt Esther made a proposal:

"A number of our nephews are at war, and I make a motion that should any of them be killed in action that the tombstones read that they had served their country during World War II."

Alice cringed. She had wanted to bring Al to this beautiful home to show him off to her family. It was only a matter of time before he would be shipped overseas. And when she looked at Aunt Yetta's ferocious face, she knew an explosion was about to occur.

"My two sons are overseas. How dare you, Esther! What do you know, you only have daughters," Yetta shrieked.

Alice glanced at Albert and could see that his eyebrows were raised, and he gave her a wan smile. She could see where this was going and tried to hold back her tears.

Riva and Chana, both with sons in the service, began screaming and crying. "Are you out of your mind, Esther, killing off our sons? Why are you assuming that our boys would be killed? Is that what you want?"

Instead of apologizing, Esther talked softly. "I'm just being realistic. There's a war going on. The law of averages; one of them could very well die."

Yetta lunged at Esther and they began to pull each other's hair. Hitting and punching followed. The other mothers of sons continued screaming and crying.

By now, Alice was ready to start screaming at her aunts. But she didn't want her newly minted fiancé to think she was an unrefined shrew like they were. She looked at him, throwing her hands up in the air. He smiled and winked at her.

Aunt Mollie, whose son was also in the military, tried to make peace, explaining that Esther had not meant what she said, but her voice was drowned out in the chaos.

Esther picked up a plate and threw it against the wall. Yetta threw a glass onto the floor, which shattered into many tiny pieces. After Moishe and Uncle Jonah separated them by force, it took several minutes before everybody quieted down.

Alice fought back tears.

Yetta and Esther sat glaring at each other for the rest of the evening while Alice, her mother, Albert, and the hostess got on their hands and knees to clean up the wreckage.

"Be careful," Al said to Alice. "Don't cut yourself on the glass."

Alice watched Albert empty a dustpan into the kitchen garbage and smirk. She feared that he was laughing at her and her insane family. Convinced that this was the beginning of the end, she was sure he was thinking that they were savages.

Since they were supposed to see each other the next day before going back to their furloughs, and since Alice was going home that night with her parents, she figured she might as well ask him point-blank.

"So are we still on for tomorrow?" she asked.

"Of course, why wouldn't we be?" he replied.

Alice suddenly felt tears build up behind her eyes as she looked at this dark, handsome, perfect specimen of a man: her fiancé.

"My family," she said. "Just so you know, they're not always like this."

To her surprise, Albert gave her a big smile.

"This is nothing," he said. "Wait until you meet my family."

4

Fighting Hitler
Alice's War

In late November 1938, my oldest cousin, Rabbi Robert Strauss, came for a visit.

"I have a big favor to ask of you," Robert, whom the family called Robbie, said to my parents in the living room of our Montclair, New Jersey, home.

"I know this is an imposition, but this is a matter of life and death," he said. "I need to place a young Jewish girl from Berlin—just about Alice's age—in a nice home, just for a short time. Germany is on fire and it's only going to get worse. After Kristallnacht, I can see what's coming. It's only going to get worse and worse for the Jews in Germany."

My cousin was a very handsome man—tall and clean-shaven with a shock of black hair and piercing blue eyes. He spoke with a powerful, booming voice and clearly articulated each word. My mother adored him because she thought all rabbis should be good-looking and speak the King's English. And he was her favorite nephew, the son of her best-loved sister, Mollie.

My father loved Robbie for many reasons, but mainly because he was a fellow Zionist, who, like him, wanted a homeland for Jews in Palestine. He was also impressed when Robbie insisted on speaking out against the Hitler regime, even throwing his support behind a boycott of German goods to protest treatment of the Jews.

When the Nazis first came to power, many thought Hitler's rhetoric and measures were temporary.

"What do you mean? What's coming?" my mother asked him.

"Look, Gisela's been forced out of her public school, where she once was a top student," the rabbi explained. "Her parents secured papers for her, but they're hesitant to come here themselves because the Nazis will strip them of their savings."

"Doesn't the girl have any close relatives in America?" my father asked.

"Yes, she does, and they are prepared to take her—just not immediately. She has an aunt and uncle in Washington Heights whose daughter will be getting married soon. The plan is that once their daughter moves out, Gisela will be able to stay in her cousin's bedroom for as long as necessary. Hopefully, her parents will decide to come soon."

My parents readily agreed, and a few weeks later, Gisela moved into our home. My mother borrowed a cot from one of her brothers and pillows, sheets, and blankets from Aunt Mollie. She set it up next to my bed and I added a teddy bear and my bride doll. I emptied a dresser drawer and made room in my closet for Gisela's clothes. When we met, I was surprised by her blond hair and blue eyes. Not only was she beautiful, but she was smart as a whip—especially in math and science. At school, she spoke English fluently, and the teachers loved her.

But every night in the darkness of my bedroom, she cried herself to sleep. She missed her parents, grandparents, two brothers, friends, piano and violin teachers, and her own bedroom with her favorite doll, Anneliese. Gisela filled my head with horror stories about neighbors turned informers, beatings and arrests of Jews for no reason, rabbis whose beards were cut off in public, and old people who were made to clean the streets with toothbrushes. And worst of all, she shared her fears that her family would not be able to get out and join her in America.

The following June, we both graduated from Montclair High School. A week later, Gisela said goodbye and went to live with her aunt and uncle. In September, I started at NYU, and Gisela went to Bryn Mawr College in Pennsylvania.

I continued to be in touch with her and with Robbie, both of whom provided me with updates about the Nazi persecution of the Jews. The news from Europe got worse and worse, and throughout the continent, Jews were in ever greater peril. Gisela, it turns out, was something of a genius. After college, she went on to graduate school, and eventually received her PhD in physics. The frightened girl who shared my bedroom ended up working on the Manhattan Project to develop an atomic bomb. But Gisela's parents couldn't get out. They had waited too long to make a move. I became obsessed with Gisela and her family, and I believed everything I heard about Nazi atrocities, even when many people thought the news was exaggerated.

Days after graduating from college, I went to see the film *Hitler's Children*, which was a big box office hit. It scared the hell out of me. It showed how Hitler rose to power by brainwashing the youth of Germany. The film confirmed everything

Robbie and Gisela had told us and everything I read in the Jewish newspapers. I knew that I had to do my part.

Days after graduation, I enlisted in the army. My father tried to stop me, begging me not to go, crying to my mother that they had already lost my eight-year-old brother to polio. "Are you out of your mind, Sadie? Do you want to risk the life of our remaining child?" He was normally a mild-mannered man, but his face turned beet red as he shouted at my mother.

Conversely—and shockingly—my mother told me I should enlist if I really wanted to. That if I didn't, I would always regret it. This made sense to me, as my mother had shared her own story of disappointment. She had told me that when she graduated from high school, she had secretly applied and been accepted to Beth Israel School of Nursing. She showed me the two-page acceptance letter, which listed all the supplies she was required to bring. Perhaps her parents couldn't afford the tuition or supplies. But they had scoffed at her lifelong dream, and my grandmother forbade her from attending, saying she was needed at home to help with the youngest of the twelve children.

"I'm not going to be like my parents, stopping you from what you want to do," my mother told me.

"This is hardly the same thing," retorted my father. "I doubt that Alice plans to make the military her career."

"No, of course not, but with a college degree, I can be an officer," I insisted. I had big dreams of working in public relations and becoming an officer.

And since I fervently believed that my military service would help defeat the Nazis, three days after I graduated, I visited the WAC recruiting office and was welcomed by an enthusiastic WAC corporal.

"You are definitely officer material," she assured me. "And there is a great need for trained public relations officers."

She told me of the wonderful job the WACs were doing and of their tremendous contribution to the war effort. She said she couldn't give me a 100 percent guarantee I would be a public relations officer, but if I signed up immediately, I probably would be granted any assignment I requested.

I listened attentively as she proposed that when initially interviewed at base I should request Officer Candidates School and not public relations officer.

"Become an officer first," she advised. "And then choose your field. That way, if public relations is not available, you can go into special services, personnel, or any of a half dozen other jobs."

Her description of life in the army was glowing—challenging jobs, many promotions, interesting associates, travel, concerts, dances. So when she suggested I fill out an application immediately, take a passport photo, and then return for a physical and a swearing-in, I eagerly complied.

The application completed, I was sent to another building and ushered into a doctor's office.

I didn't like the internist, who took my blood pressure, listened to my heart and lungs, and then requested I drop the robe and bend over—once, twice, and then again as he walked to the other end of the room to study me in my naked, bent-over position. I felt degraded.

There was a definite sneer on his face as he asked me if I had ever had sexual relations. I thought to myself: *What am I getting into? What kind of exam is this? What kind of question is he asking? Why is this his business? Is this type of behavior really a part of his job, or is he just a lech? I can tell he thinks all WACs are tramps.*

As he asked me to lie down on the table and put my feet in the stirrups for the internal, I began to think that I should get up and walk out, that I was making a terrible mistake. This was my first exposure to the Women's Army Corps and already a misogynistic man was leering at me instead of showing me respect for wanting to serve my country during a time of war.

Despite my trepidations, after the exam I returned to the recruiting headquarters as instructed. With the worst over, my apprehension began to fade and I became infused again with the wish to do my share against the Nazis.

I raised my arm and took the oath to defend my country. I was now a member of the Women's Army Corps awaiting orders. But I soon found out that promises made in recruitment are not necessarily kept.

At the beginning of July, I boarded a train in Newark for my basic training at Fort Devens in Massachusetts, where I was assigned to a lower bunk with a hard mattress. The girls in my barracks included a nurse, a home economics associate professor, a music teacher, and a secretary. They were friendly and upbeat.

On the first day, we had a breakfast of cereal and prunes and pancakes in syrup—everything on one tray. *What a mess,* I thought. *No wonder it's called* mess.

Then we marched. Left face, right face, about face. Pivot on the heel; pivot on the toe. Salute. Straighten the arm. Straighten the hand. My head was spinning as I tried to follow the instructions.

At lunchtime, the sergeant gave us instructions. "Do not request anything you are not going to eat. You must—and I repeat *must*—eat everything on your tray."

Our first lunch, all offered on one tray—potatoes, carrots, spinach, pork chops, and baked raisin pie—looked disgusting.

The potatoes were lumpy, the carrots and spinach floated around in greasy water, the pork chops were hard and dry; but I was hungry. Thankfully, I accepted everything except for the pork chops. But what had I been thinking before I enlisted? It had never occurred to me that in the army I would no longer have kosher meat.

As we stacked our trays when the meal was finished, I heard a disturbance. It was Elizabeth, the home economics associate professor, arguing. In her thirties, she had a regal look about her—tall, elegant, intelligent with a quiet, commanding manner. The first time I saw her, I thought that she was bound to end up an officer.

"Return to your seat immediately," the sergeant demanded of Elizabeth, "and finish your lunch."

"I can't," Elizabeth replied. "I almost vomited trying to eat. I really can't eat this, especially now. The spinach is cold and the pork chops are dry and hard and greasy."

"Tough," said the sergeant. "You're going to have to. In fact, you will remain in this mess hall all night, if necessary, until you do."

Elizabeth later told me that she had stuffed the food in her pockets when the sergeant wasn't looking.

After lunch, we were given a test to determine our assignments, and later in the afternoon we were interviewed.

"I see you have typing skills," the lieutenant said. "Is there some particular field you would like to work in?"

"I want to go to Officer Candidates School," I said.

She looked at me as if I had three heads. I could see that she thought I was out of my mind. What was going on? When I enlisted, I had been encouraged to believe that with my college degree, I would be an officer.

"OCS is overcrowded. In what field would you like to work?"

"I want to be an officer," I insisted.

"Just forget it," the lieutenant told me. "You are here to serve. I suggest you tell me what field you would like to do your stenography in. If after you receive your stripes you still want OCS, you can apply."

That was it. I was dismissed. This was not the picture that recruitment had painted. But I still held out hope. Perhaps this lieutenant didn't have the final word.

The days in basic training rolled by. Clean the barracks, make the beds, scrub the latrine, report for kitchen patrol (KP), march, drill, and attend classes. We received our uniforms and supplies. We marched again and again—morning and afternoon—covering most of the forty-nine square miles of Fort Devens. The stiff leather of the high shoes used for marching rubbed our heels and big toes, creating tremendous, painful blisters.

But I told myself over and over again, *I'm sacrificing for my country. This is my contribution in helping to make our world free.*

Almost daily we were shown films—lucid, horrible, vivid portrayals of the German invasion—but the one that will remain with me forever was the ghastly picture of the Germans piling naked bodies into mountains and shoveling them into mass graves. As I sat watching that film, the tears streaming down my cheeks, I was proud that I had joined the army, proud that I was serving.

The next day on KP, I brought extra vigor to my tête-à-tête with the bottoms of the garbage cans. No matter how trivial my contribution, I was helping win this war. I scrubbed not only the garbage cans but also tables, benches, and floors hard and fast.

In August, we were formally inducted into the army and received our redeployment assignments. I was going to be sent to Fort Belvoir in Virginia, outside of Washington, DC. But first there was a long and arduous train ride in a sweltering old coach car with hard wooden seats and no washroom. When we finally reached the hills, the mountains, and the crisp cool air of Virginia, only six hours from my home in New Jersey, it felt glorious.

The next day we waited in line in the hallway of post headquarters for our interviews. I saluted the captain and sat down. She said, "You will be a clerk-typist for a major."

I swallowed hard. I knew that it was now or never; this was the time to speak. "Ma'am, I had hoped to get into public relations."

"What is there about public relations that interests everybody?" she asked. "You're the fifth one asking for it this morning."

"Ma'am, I don't know about the others. But I do know that I spent five years going to college at night so I could be something more than a secretary."

She hesitated at first, but then said, "I'll have the captain in public relations interview you."

I was sent to the PR office, where I was instructed to write a lede on one of the office typewriters for an article on the contributions of the WACs to the war effort. There were three men watching me: a captain, a lieutenant, and a corporal. I was shaking. I took so long trying to come up with an outstanding lede that the captain and lieutenant lost interest and returned to their desks.

I wrote one line. The corporal looked at it and said, "I think you've got what we want. How about going into that other room by yourself? Write the whole article and a feature story on how the WAC keeps beautiful."

I took an hour and a half. I gave the feature story an emotional pitch—I wrote about the pride within the WAC that makes her glow, the shining future reflected in her eyes. When I was finished, it crossed my mind that no man would ever be asked to write a story about how the GIs stay handsome. But I gave them what I thought they wanted.

And apparently it was. I got the job. I was immediately asked to interview a WAC serving in the kitchen who, with both her son and husband in service, was celebrating her silver wedding anniversary on KP. And then I was sent to the service club and the library to write articles on foods and the club's new furniture.

During the next several days, I learned that the editor of the *Belvoir Castle* was hospitalized. The corporal who had worked for the Associated Press before induction was the only writer on the staff, so I was desperately needed.

The many stories I was told to cover held a tremendous fascination for me. I was impressed with this job. The *Belvoir Castle*—with a circulation of ten thousand—was the official camp newspaper. I had never before spoken with so many different types of people. I was awed.

I sent a picture of myself in my WAC uniform to Gisela. I was now officially part of the United States Armed Forces. Whatever I was asked to do, I would do my part in defeating the Nazis.

5
Guinea Pig

It was a beautiful spring day, a week after Passover, and the memories of the Gildner Family Circle Seder were still dancing in Alice's head. Her daughter, Marjorie, was turning seven years old soon, and it had been her turn to recite the Four Questions to the eighty relatives assembled at the Hotel Diplomat in Manhattan for the family's annual Seder. Marjorie had received accolades from not only her parents, but also the many aunts and uncles and cousins. Esther, her older cousin, led her to the hidden afikomen and told her that it was hers because she had done such a great job. She was to give the afikomen to Robbie, the family rabbi, when everyone finished with dinner so he could continue with the second half of the Seder. And she would get her prize: a copy of *Charlotte's Web*. Alice could see that her daughter felt grown up receiving a book as a present, although one that dealt with death might have to be put on the shelf for a while.

The Easter-Passover school vacation would be over in a couple of days, and Alice was anxious to get Marjorie out of the house and breathe in the fresh air. Besides, it was the anniversary of her brother's death, who had succumbed to polio as a child. She needed to clear her head.

"Let's go for a walk and look at the spring flowers," Alice said to her daughter. Her older son Barry was playing around the corner with some friends, and her husband, Al, was at work. Alice loved to garden and enjoyed ordering seeds each year when Marjorie's school held a PTA fundraiser. She loved planting them, even getting her hands dirty, but most of all, watching them grow.

She also enjoyed seeing what the neighbors did to beautify their forty-by-one-hunded-feet pieces of property. As they walked down the street of neat little brick Cape Cods built close together, Alice pointed out the blooming spring flowers to her daughter.

"Look at those beautiful tulips around the Rossis' porch. What colors do you see?"

"I see red and yellow and pink and white."

"And look at the yellow daffodils," Alice pointed out. "Remember when you were a yellow daffodil in kindergarten and Robert Mondschein was the gardener? I was afraid he was going to rake your head off."

"I wasn't afraid, Mommy, it was pretend. My costume was made of yellow crepe paper and Robert had a toy rake."

Suddenly, Bertha Balsam came barreling out of her house with a scowl on her face as she motioned for them to stop. The wrinkles in her forehead accentuated her bushy black eyebrows and her long black hair. Bertha was a big woman, and she threw her weight around. She had an opinion about everything and wasn't afraid to voice it. Although Marjorie sometimes played with Bertha's daughter, Gwen, she was a little afraid of Bertha. Marjorie's best friend, Denise Rossi, had whispered to her that Bertha might be a communist. This frightened Marjorie even though she had no idea what a communist was.

"Did you return the permission letter to the school allowing Marjorie to be in the Salk polio vaccine field trial?" Bertha bellowed in full attack mode. "Of course, I've signed Gwen up. It's such an honor that they're having it at PS 347. There'll be 1.8 million students in the United States, Canada, and Finland participating in the trials. And to think, they're including our kids. But we won't know whether each child will be getting an inoculation or a placebo."

Alice said nothing. She looked at her daughter and saw the concern on her face and knew that Marjorie was waiting for her to respond. Marjorie looked at her mother and wondered why she was speechless. Why wasn't she answering Mrs. Balsam?

"So did you return the permission slip?"

"I'm not giving permission. I don't want her in the trial," Alice finally replied.

"What do you mean you don't want her in the trial? It's our patriotic duty to help stamp out polio."

Bertha began to raise her voice.

Alice knew that Bertha was a big advocate for the polio vaccine, but she was not prepared for her neighbor's wrath. And she was uncomfortable that she was starting this debate in front of Marjorie. Alice was the kind of mother who did her best to shield her children from unpleasant adult conversations.

"I don't want my child to be a guinea pig," she finally blurted out in exasperation.

"Guinea pig—are you nuts? They wouldn't be giving it to almost two million children if there was any danger."

"How can you be so sure? They wouldn't call it a trial if they knew for sure it was perfectly safe. How do you know they won't get polio from it or perhaps have some long-term effects?"

Alice didn't tell her that she had spoken with her friend and neighbor Connie Murphy, who was a registered nurse and said she wasn't going to allow her daughter, Louisa, to be in the trials either.

Bertha pointed her finger at Alice and moved closer to her, so close Alice could feel her breath on her. She raised her voice: "It's narrow-minded people like you who stand in the way of progress. It's your patriotic duty! You should be ashamed of yourself."

The words *patriotic duty* rankled Alice. After all, Alice was a veteran of World War II. She had enlisted in the army the same week she graduated from college. Bertha had not served her country or attended college. But she considered herself to be an expert on everything and wore a mantle of righteousness on whatever side of an issue she argued. Still, Alice, decided not to go there.

"People have their reasons. And you should mind your own business," Alice responded. "Let's go, Marjorie."

Alice took her confused daughter by the hand as they walked away and approached Union Turnpike, where stores were located. "How about we get some ice cream?" she said.

"Okay, Mommy, but why don't you want me to have the polio shot?"

Alice could feel her heart pounding and she felt short of breath. How dare Bertha the buttinsky make her explain this to her not-yet-seven-year-old daughter?

"I want to keep you perfectly safe. I don't want to take any chances."

"But why?"

"You know how Grandma always mentions my brother, Bernie. He caught polio, then got pneumonia and died."

"How old was he?"

"Eight."

"I'll be eight next year. But everyone else in our class except me and Louisa are getting the shot. I don't want to die from polio."

"As soon as I know it's perfectly safe and approved, I promise you'll get it, but I don't want you in an experiment. To me, it feels like it's too much of a risk. Sometimes, we must think for ourselves and not go along with the crowd."

That night after Marjorie and Barry were tight asleep and Alice and her husband Al were in bed, he asked her what was wrong.

"You've been in another world since I got home from work," Albert observed. "What's the matter, honey? What's going on?"

"It's that busybody, Bertha Balsam."

"I told you to stay away from her."

"She practically attacked me on the street."

"About what this time? Who or what is she campaigning for now?"

"In front of Marjorie, she attacked me for not allowing her to be in the polio vaccine trials."

"None of her business," he said.

"I know," Alice began to cry.

Albert switched off the television. "Talk to me."

"You know, this is still difficult for me," she said. "I understand from my mother that for the first year of my life I was a cute, chubby baby and that we were the ideal American family until my brother contracted polio when he was five. Every day, my mother told me that she carried him onto trolley cars to bring him to a polio clinic, where he could be treated. She said she left me with anybody who was willing to watch me for a few hours. My memory begins when I was about three and I can see him walking, though he had his legs in braces."

Alice remembered the layout of their dark three-room first-floor apartment in the Bronx, where Bernie slept in the living room on a couch that opened. Alice slept in a crib in the bedroom with her parents. Each morning, before breakfast, she would dash into the living room, pounce onto the couch, and unbuckle her brother's braces. She recalled standing in front of their apartment watching the young boys play games of marbles. Bernie couldn't bend, so he would lean against the wall with her and watch.

"Actually, by the time I was four, my brother's condition improved and there was even talk of dispensing with home tutoring and sending him to school the following September."

In the middle of April after he had a bath, Bernie became chilled. The doctors diagnosed pneumonia. Alice's mother still felt guilty for giving him a bath. She said he just didn't have any resistance because of the polio.

"He died a couple of weeks later—on a beautiful day like today."

"Oh, Alice," Albert said with tears in his eyes.

"My mother told me that he was in heaven with God. She said that there are other little boys there and he will be happy, but I remember feelings of despair and anger. 'If God has other boys, he doesn't have to take my brother. It isn't fair. I want him! I want him!' I cried and cried."

"Bertha is a creep," Albert said, then made the face he always made before he said something he knew might be hurtful. "Don't get upset with me, but just explain that if your brother died from polio, you don't want Marjorie to get the vaccine."

"I didn't say she couldn't get the vaccine." Alice rolled her eyes and raised her voice. "I said I didn't want her to be a guinea pig in an experiment. A trial is just that; they're testing it out to see what happens. Once it's proven safe—that there are no side effects, and it doesn't bring on the disease—she can get it."

"Fair enough," Albert said as he held her close. "But stay away from Bertha. She's a know-it-all bully."

"I will."

Alice was relieved that Albert always supported her decisions, especially where the children were concerned, but it was not lost on her that she needed to explain her position to him.

And while Alice thought the best time for Marjorie to read *Charlotte's Web* would have been in a year or two, she began to think that maybe they should read it together now. For one thing, Marjorie was excited about the new book, and Alice wanted to foster her love of reading. And the book was all about friendship, love, life, and death, which, after all, had been her family's story ever since her memory began.

A year later, when the vaccine was deemed safe, Marjorie and her brother Barry and the Murphy sisters lined up in alphabetical order with their respective classes at PS 347 to be jabbed in the arm with the polio vaccine.

By then, Bertha Balsam had a new cause and new targets to attack. Still, Alice remained troubled by the incident. Why were the health decisions she made for her children any business of others?

After the vaccine basically eradicated polio in the United States, Alice second-guessed her decision not to allow Marjorie in the trial. It was not lost on her that she had had to explain her thinking to Albert about why she had not been willing to gamble with her own child's health and safety. The image of her brother in braces, and her mother's constant invoking of his memory, remained in her heart.

Now that both of her children were immunized, Alice was relieved. She appreciated the parents of the 1.8 million children who had participated in the Salk vaccine trials.

While the specter of polio faded from the newspapers and from the concerns of American parents, the memory of her brother standing at the front window of their apartment watching the other boys play marbles would stay with her forever.

6

After the War

The scent of brownies—brownie batter, brownies baking, brownies hot from the oven, and brownies cooling—filled Alice's tiny kitchen and indeed every corner of her small Cape Cod.

The brownies were best right out of the oven, and Alice cut off a piece and let it melt in her mouth. The aroma even wafted upstairs to the finished attic where Marjorie and Barry had their bedrooms. Alice's secret ingredient was the chocolate chips that gave the brownies more sweetness, heft, and that melt-in-your-mouth quality that everyone loved. She supposed that was why she had been assigned the task of baking brownies for the annual school bake sale.

While Alice was flattered that everyone loved her brownies, now that both of her children were in school full-time, she had begun to think about what she was doing with her life. Like the vast majority of other mothers in her neighborhood, she was a stay-at-home mom. But she remembered wistfully that once she had not been afraid to march to the beat of her own drum— both figuratively and literally. The week she graduated from college, she had enlisted in the US Army, determined to do her part to fight the Nazi menace.

Just as she stuffed another brownie into her mouth, her next-door neighbor Connie Murphy, interrupting her thoughts, appeared at the side door, which opened directly into the kitchen. Connie was petite, five feet, slim, with blond hair, a turned-up nose, and blue eyes. She was wearing her crisp white nurse's uniform—starched and pristine with white stockings, white lace-up oxfords, and a white pillbox hat.

"Are you coming or going?" Alice asked.

"I'm coming from the high school. They called me this morning. The regular nurse was out sick, and they needed someone to substitute for the day."

"How did that go?"

"Fine, just the usual. Stomach viruses, a basketball injury, a paper cut."

"How are the apple crumb cakes coming?"

"I've made six already and I'll make six more tonight."

"Do you have time for a cup of coffee before the kids are home?"

"That would be great, thanks."

They sat down at the white chrome kitchen table in the tiny dinette area, where Alice poured two cups of coffee and put some brownies on a plate.

"So, I've been thinking, Connie. I've just spent the better part of two days making brownies, and you've been making crumb cakes in between working as a substitute nurse. Our kids are getting older, they're in school all day. What are we doing with our lives?"

"I guess what we've always done since we got married, what we're expected to do—cooking, cleaning, raising kids, making sure our husbands have everything they need so they can support us."

"But look at you in your uniform, so professional," said Alice. "It really suits you. And at least you're doing something. But you could do so much more. Do you ever think about your war experience?"

"I think about it all the time," said Connie. "I believe I made a difference to the soldiers I treated and comforted. I felt like I was doing it for my brother and his comrades. But there was nothing that can compare to being at Dachau. What I saw still keeps me awake at night."

Connie had been a nurse in World War II and, after serving in various countries, was part of the team that liberated Dachau.

Alice had been stationed at Fort Belvoir outside of the nation's capital.

"You're a college graduate, Alice. You're smart. You do such a great job with the PTA newsletter. Did you ever think you wanted to do more than be a housewife?"

"Sure, I had dreams, but above all, I wanted a family. And I've been blessed with Al and two beautiful kids. It takes all of my time to take care of them."

"The kids are getting older, Alice, and surely Al can pitch in. My husband feeds the kids when I sub at the hospital on the four-through-twelve shift."

"Why did you join the military, Connie?"

"My brother was in the army, and I wanted to be there for him and his fellow soldiers. What about you?"

"I enrolled days after I graduated from NYU. I had seen a film called *Hitler's Children* and it seemed like the right thing to do. The movie was about how Hitler rose to power by brainwashing the young people of Germany and turning them against their parents. I was horrified. And of course, there were no men around; they were all in the army," Alice added with a slightly mischievous smile.

"Are you sorry you did it?"

"Look, it was an experience, but I honestly don't see how I made that much of a difference to the war effort. It toughened me up. I did KP, I remember cleaning out a big vat of grease, and it spilled all over the floor and I had to clean it up myself. I still gag when I think of it. I learned physical endurance, marching for miles in basic training. It expanded my horizons beyond the metropolitan area. I bonded with girls who had never met a Jew before. I became close friends with lesbians. And I guess I interviewed several notable people, including Eleanor Roosevelt and Rabbi Stephen Wise."

"Wasn't Rabbi Wise the one who had Roosevelt's ear?"

"That's what they say, what he said. But they didn't want to use my story. I was hoping it would appear in *Stars and Stripes*, but they weren't interested in that angle. They were focused on winning the war, like the president. FDR was intent on winning the war, not rescuing Jews while it was going on. I suppose he tried. But there were egos involved."

"There always are."

"But what about you, Connie? Would you do it again?"

"I would," she said. "I loved those men who suffered and died for our country, and I'm glad I was able to help them."

"And what about Dachau?" Alice asked.

"I don't know how to put it into words. When we first arrived and walked along the street, there were gorgeous trees there. But when I turned the corner, all I could see were dead bodies piled upon each other. The stench was awful.

"When I went over to the survivors and said I was an American nurse they were so happy. They clapped and smiled, but they were all walking skeletons.

"When I walked into the barracks I was assigned to, there was a girl who looked about ten years old with gray hair lying on the cot. She didn't know what was going on. They had removed her appendix without giving her anesthesia."

"When you came home, did you discuss what you had seen?"

"Not so much. No one really wanted to hear about it. And the enlisted men just wanted to return to their lives—get married, buy a house, have children. Everyone just wanted to move on. But there was one incident that happened to me shortly after I came home. I had gone to the beauty parlor after not cutting my hair for what felt like years, and a woman I knew from school came over to me while I was under the dryer. We had been in the same classes and her family went to the same church as mine. But we had never been friends.

"She came and stood in front of me, and she was scowling. She said to me, 'I don't believe that there were all those killings over there, and that there were concentration camps and that the Jews suffered as much as they're saying.'

"I pushed my dryer back and I jumped up. I said, 'You better believe they were dying, and that they suffered as much as everybody says they did. I was there.'

"She never answered. She just turned on her heels and stomped out. But everybody around heard me."

"People don't want to talk about it—you saw that for yourself," Alice said. "It defies imagination that it happened, but it's heartbreaking that there are Americans who don't believe it. Oh, Connie, how did the world allow this to happen?"

"I don't know. Indifference, selfishness, lack of attention, antisemitism—I could go on and on."

"Has anything changed?" Alice asked.

"I don't know. We defeated Hitler, but there are still haters among us."

"Do you ever think about what we're doing with our lives now—baking brownies and crumb cakes?"

"Well," said Connie. "I'm seriously thinking about getting a full-time nursing job; there are only so many apple crumb cakes I can make."

"I sometimes think I could get a job," said Alice. "Maybe as a reporter for a local newspaper or a job in public relations. But the only mother who works is Gloria Benson, and that's because she's a widow. I feel like I should be here when my kids come home from school."

"But don't they go to Hebrew School?"

"They do, but I like to give them a snack before they go. Maybe when the kids are in junior high in a couple of years."

"We really need to continue this conversation another time. I've got to get going. The kids will be home soon."

Alice took two brownies out of one of the cooling pans and wrapped them in aluminum foil. "Here, take these for the road."

"Thanks," Connie said. "I'll see you at the bake sale tomorrow."

7

The Nazi House

Although Lilli Sternberger was plain, she exuded confidence. That made her an object of curiosity—and even jealousy—for Marjorie when they were growing up in Queens. Their homes, mirror images of one another, were set back to back with small patches of green grass, an apple tree, a rock garden and concrete patios, and a chain-link fence between them. Lilli was a popular girl from the time she and her sister, Heidi, moved to Bellerose. Lilli was in the third grade and Heidi was in the fifth.

On the playground at PS 347, Lilli surrounded herself with a posse of ostensibly pretty and popular girls, whom she chose for their loyalty and deference to her. Marjorie longed to be in Lilli's inner circle, but she couldn't quite figure out how to be accepted by the group, not having the nerve to ask. So she just watched the girls from afar, fascinated and impressed by their self-confidence and importance. It would be incorrect to say that she was one of the unfortunate girls who Lilli and her friends actively singled out for exclusion and bullying. Indeed, she was invited to their birthday parties.

But she just wasn't in the exclusive four-member "in-crowd" she so desperately wanted to join.

Marjorie was convinced that Lilli led a charmed life. The other kids talked about how rich her father was. He owned three dry-cleaning stores, and rumor was that he was about to open a fourth. The family owned a black Lincoln Continental, went to Florida every winter and to the Jersey Shore in the summer. When mohair sweaters became popular, Lilli had one in a different color for every day of the week. When charm bracelets became the rage, Marjorie observed that Lilli had a bracelet that was so filled with gold charms that there were no spaces for more.

"Other people's lives look perfect when you're on the outside looking in. But no one's life is perfect when you're on the inside," Alice told her daughter. "Anyway, how would you like to have a sister like Heidi? Lilli is a *mieskeit* and Heidi is stunning."

"I wish I had a sister; I've been asking you to have another baby for years now."

"I told you there's no guarantee that I wouldn't have another boy. And besides, I'm too old now."

"You don't look old," said Marjorie, who was now fifteen.

"And it's exhausting," said her mother. "The diapers and formula and getting up in the middle of the night. I don't want you to be a built-in babysitter. You're on the cusp of so many exciting adventures."

Marjorie knew that this was likely true. And it was impossible to go back in time and have an older sister. She was resigned to the fact that her brother, Barry, who was two years older than she, would be her only sibling. Barry was all right; they got along well, but she couldn't discuss girly things with him.

Nevertheless, no matter what her mother said, Marjorie believed deep in her heart that Lilli was at an advantage because of her older sister.

When they entered high school, Lilli began to look better. It was clear to Marjorie that it must have been Heidi who had transformed Lilli's appearance by teaching her how to apply makeup, brightening up her pale skin and lackluster features, and enhancing her brown eyes with black liquid eyeliner and mascara. And the mousy brown kinky hair of elementary-school days was now gone—likely straightened and colored at Heidi's suggestion. While Lilli as a child had been the homely spitting image of her rich and powerful father, she was now a refined and attractive version.

Marjorie also observed that Lilli never seemed to have a shortage of boys flocking around her. There was a coquettish quality she had—she smiled and giggled in a flirtatious way. Marjorie, on the other hand, was shy, anxious, and introverted. She credited Lilli's sister for paving the way for her. There was no one—save her mother and grandmother—who cared about Marjorie enough to tell her what she could do to attract boys. And their advice was stuck in previous generations.

Oh, how she wished she had a sister like Heidi! Lilli and her sister didn't look alike. Heidi had long and silky flaxen hair and piercing blue eyes. While Lilli looked like she might be a good candidate for a nose job and had even mentioned her plans to have one when she turned sixteen, Heidi's nose was small and turned up. In fact, while Lilli resembled her father, Heidi didn't take after either of her parents. Her mother, Elsa, while quite attractive in her own right, had auburn hair and dark brown eyes.

When they first moved into the neighborhood, neighbors speculated that perhaps Heidi was adopted, perhaps a war orphan. But that rumor soon got squashed when Elsa shared her tragic experience during World War II in Europe. She had made clear in the telling that this would be the one and only time she would speak about it; her experience had been so unspeakably heinous and she could not relive it each time a neighbor inquired. So, it was left to the original listeners to pass her harrowing tale to the other neighbors. And as human beings are prone to do, they perhaps shared it with some embellishment.

The story in its barest outlines was that Elsa was born in Germany to a wealthy Jewish family, but they were deported to Poland by the Nazis. Being exiled to the despair and disease and filth of the Warsaw Ghetto, Elsa's parents and her younger siblings died there. She, however, had hidden in the sewers during the liquidation of the ghetto. Somehow, she hooked up with partisans in the forest, where she lived out the war in a bunker, married one of the partisan leaders, and got pregnant. Unfortunately, her husband was killed days before liberation. Her baby girl, Heidi, was born in June 1945 when Elsa was twenty-three.

Elsa said that she brought Heidi to the United States after the war and met Lou, an ambitious World War II veteran, when she walked into his first dry-cleaning store in Flushing. A few months later, he married her and adopted Heidi. Initially, they lived in an apartment in Flushing, and when Elsa got pregnant with Lilli, they moved to Bellerose.

When the girls were small, and groups of children gathered on the street, Marjorie and Lilli would join with other kids to play Red Light, Green Light and Ringolevio. Later, their paths crossed in high school classes and at boy-girl parties in the neighborhood kids' finished basements, where 45 rpm records would play with the lights turned low. The teenage boys and girls would cling close to one another to a slow dance.

Marjorie had been invited to Lilli's backyard birthday parties, and whenever she rang the bell for Lilli, she was invited in. While all the homes in the neighborhood were the same, Lilli's parents had enlarged theirs in the front, adding a dining room, in the back with a den, and upstairs with two bedrooms and a bathroom for Lilli and Heidi. Lilli's bedroom was a sea of lavender with lace curtains, a white kidney-shaped dressing table covered in a sheer lavender material with a mirror on top, and a lavender bedspread with purple orchids scattered about. To Marjorie, who didn't have a big basis of comparison, their home looked big and beautiful and flawless, as well it should, since the perfect family lived there. And Marjorie thought that Princess Anne herself might be at home in Lilli's bedroom.

When Marjorie and Lilli were sophomores in high school, they were both in the same honors social studies class. The teacher, Mrs. Bernstein, had given them an assignment to interview their parents about their experiences during World War II. The first task was to craft the questions they would ask their mother or father. Mrs. Bernstein spent a whole period on how to ask questions like, *What did you do in the war?* Of course, Marjorie's father, Albert, had served in the US Army during the war. But so had her mother, Alice, unlike most women her age who supported the war effort by working in factories and taking on other traditionally male occupations. Another exception was Rosemary Murphy's mom, Connie, who was an army nurse in Europe.

The week Marjorie's mom graduated from college after seeing the film *Hitler's Children*, she enlisted in the Women's Army Corps. She had told Marjorie about her personal experience working on the army newspaper, marching, and cleaning out huge vats of grease as part of her KP stint, but not about the questions Marjorie had in mind to ask: *Were the world and governments aware of what was happening to the Jews of Europe? Was it written about in the newspapers? What did you know? Did you write about it? If so, how did everyone allow six million Jews to be murdered? Should/could the United States have done anything to stop it? What is our responsibility to our fellow human beings? Do you think it can happen again?*

The next day, Mrs. Bernstein asked the students to share the questions they planned to ask their parents. Fred Hanson's father had been on a navy submarine, and Fred wanted to know what that was like. *Was his father afraid all the time? Did he ever come close to losing his life? Did his experience bear any similarity to the sailors in* The Caine Mutiny? Carol Smith's dad was in the Pacific when Hiroshima was bombed. *Did he think about the civilians who were killed or was he just relieved that the war ended?*

And then there was Lilli Sternberger, who everyone suspected would have the best interview of all. *What was it like to grow up rich in Germany and then be expelled because you were Jewish? What were the worst things you saw/experienced in the Warsaw Ghetto? How did it feel to lose your entire family? How long were you in the forest with the partisans?*

Mrs. Bernstein made suggestions to each of the students' questions, and it was apparent to Marjorie that her teacher was pleased with the progress of the assignment. Years later when Marjorie became a teacher herself, she thought back to this project, realizing that it was good teaching to have student-centered lessons such as this, but also a break for Mrs. Bernstein, who would spend weeks listening to the students' presentations. She gave the students two weeks to interview and prepare their reports.

"Before I assign speaking slots, is there anyone who wants to go first?"

Lilli's hand shot up. Marjorie was not surprised; Lilli was confident, almost to the point of being conceited, she thought.

"Okay, then Lilli will go first. Are there any other volunteers before I make the assignments?"

A couple of boys raised their hands. Marjorie assumed they had heroic stories to tell about their fathers. She didn't care where she ended up in the placement because she knew that her story was unique.

"I'll post the schedule tomorrow, but you can get started right away. I'm proud of your questions and I'm sure that you will each have an interview that will help us to better understand World War II."

On the day Lilli was scheduled to present her report, she was absent from school. And it was clear to Marjorie that Mrs. Bernstein had not been informed ahead of time. She even asked the students if any of them had spoken with Lilli since yesterday. And nobody had. She looked agitated and even had to improvise a lesson because Jim Conway, the second student scheduled to speak, said he wasn't ready to share his interview. He hadn't brought his father's medals and other paraphernalia with him to class that day as part of his presentation.

Mrs. Bernstein asked the class about their experiences conducting the interviews with their parents and she was able to sustain the conversation for the class period.

But what happened to Lilli? Marjorie wondered. Lilli was so full of confidence that she had volunteered to go first.

Clearly she was excited to share her mother's story. Marjorie decided to call Lilli when school was finished for the day. When Marjorie arrived home, the house was empty and she ran up to her bedroom and grabbed her pink princess phone, dialing Lilli's number. It rang once, twice. She let it ring ten times and hung up.

That's odd, perhaps she's at the doctor.

Every ten minutes for the next two hours, she tried the number, and the result was the same—no answer.

She began to hear voices downstairs; her brother Barry came in from basketball practice, her mother opened the refrigerator, then called upstairs: "Marjorie, are you up there?"

"Yes, just have to make a call; I'll be right down."

Her father arrived home for dinner. It was now dark and still no answer. Marjorie made her way downstairs to the kitchen.

"So, how was school today?" Alice asked as she checked her meatloaf in the oven.

"Strange," said Marjorie.

"How so?"

"Lilli was supposed to give her report on her mother's experience during World War II. She was the first one in the class to present and she didn't show up."

"Maybe she's sick."

"I've been calling her for hours and there's no answer. You would think her mother would have called the school to say she wasn't coming."

"Well, maybe there's a family emergency and her mother didn't think to do it. I hope they're all okay."

"Yeah, maybe," Marjorie said, but in her heart of hearts, she didn't believe it. She had a feeling deep in the pit of her stomach that something was very wrong—that they were not all right.

"Well, why don't you wait and see if she shows up for school tomorrow?"

Lilli didn't show up for school the next day, nor the day after that. Marjorie continued to call and so did others, but there was still no answer. She heard that a couple of parents who lived around the corner rang the bell and banged on the door. But no one answered.

Rumors began to make the rounds. About a week later, one neighbor shared that she had seen Lilli's father leave the house at seven in the morning and get into his car. She believed that this was proof that he was still living there by himself.

The most popular rumor was that the school district's attendance officer went to one of Mr. Sternberger's dry-cleaning stores to inquire what had happened to Lilli.

"Her mother took her," he was said to have responded.

"Will she be coming back to school?"

"No, I don't think so."

"Where did they go?"

"Your guess is as good as mine."

The story was passed from one neighbor to the next for years, although no one could be located who actually admitted to speaking to the truant officer or to Mr. Sternberger.

Eventually, he moved to Great Neck, remarried, and opened a fourth dry-cleaning store.

When a new family moved into the house, they were told the story. After all, didn't they have a right to know? And over the years, they embellished it since it had now become their story to tell.

The gossip abounded for years and there were a myriad of theories.

One suggested that Lilli's mother took her daughters to Las Vegas with her to live with her lover.

Another theory posited that either Heidi or Lilli was pregnant, and that's why they fled.

But the most popular urban legend that endured was also the most outlandish: that her father had heard Lilli interviewing her mother for the class assignment, during which she revealed to Lilli that Heidi had not been born in a bunker, but instead in a beautiful home in Germany. For the first time, Mr. Sternberger concluded that Heidi must have been the child of a Nazi officer.

It made Marjorie sad that everyone started referring to Lilli's former home as *the Nazi House*. She still thought about Lilli's lavender bedroom, dressing table, curtains, and bedspread. It had looked like a beautiful American home. And in her mind, Lilli was the closest thing to a princess she had ever encountered.

She remembered how Heidi had transformed Lilli's appearance. How fortunate was Lilli to have such a sister? She clearly cared about Lilli in a way that Marjorie realized she would never know—having only her brother, Barry. Mostly, she thought about Mr. Sternberger a lot. She wondered, if her own father had discovered something from her mother's past, would he have thrown her out so unceremoniously or would he have given her a chance to explain? Maybe Lilli's father was the heartless person here. Or he just couldn't get over that she had lied to him at the beginning. She hoped her father would not be so unforgiving.

Perhaps Lilli's mother did what she did because it was the only way she could survive in an impossible, horrific, unimaginable situation, Marjorie thought. She hadn't been a murderer herself, although her former lover was alleged to be one.

Every time the subject came up over the years, Alice would say to Marjorie: "Remember how envious you were of Lilli. You see, you never know what goes on in someone else's life."

And the more Marjorie learned about the Holocaust, the more her heart broke for Lilli's mother, who was likely just trying to stay alive.

8

Alice Gets a Job

"Anybody home?" Connie Murphy called out as she knocked on Alice's side door that opened into the kitchen. All the houses on the block were identical brick Cape Cods, and Connie lived next door. The slim, petite, five-foot neighbor was Alice's best friend on the street. They both had children who were the same ages, and they had served their country in World War II.

Connie, who had taken a full-time job two years ago at the nearby hospital, was wearing her nurse's uniform and had a book in her hand. It was 1964.

"Hi, Connie, come in. What's going on? Have you been able to see Dotty yet?" Alice asked as she looked up from the sink where she was washing dishes.

Dotty was their mutual friend who lived around the corner. She had three children, two of whom were in the same grades with their kids. Dotty was currently hospitalized with sepsis that developed after she and her sister attempted a botched abortion on her kitchen table using a coat hanger. She had required an emergency hysterectomy.

"Thankfully she's going to make it, but it was touch and go for a while," Connie said.

"I can't imagine what she was thinking to do that to herself, and with her sister helping her?"

"It's not that uncommon," Connie said. "Women are desperate. We see it in the hospital all the time. Women should be allowed to decide if and when they want to have a child. She was overwhelmed with the three she has; Bobby is only two and very active. She simply didn't want another child at this time. Now the choice has been made for her; she won't be able to have any more children."

"But she's going to be okay, right?"

"She should recover physically, but the psychological scars, who knows how long they will last."

"So sad," said Alice.

"Our country is really backward in this regard. Abortions are legal in Sweden, Norway, Puerto Rico, and even the Soviet Union. We really need a law."

"Can I call her?"

"I know she appreciates how supportive you've been. I would wait a couple days and then give her a call."

"Okay," said Alice. "I'll do that."

"I'm off to work now, but I brought you a book. You must read it. You'll find it very mind-opening."

"I didn't know you had time to read," Alice replied as she extended her hand to take the book.

"This book is a must for every woman. It's called *The Feminine Mystique* and was published last year, just nine months before JFK's assassination."

"What's it about?"

"It's about unhappy suburban housewives, how they're filled with rage because they've been forced to define themselves solely by their husbands and children. Betty Friedan writes about how women have been infantilized in American culture, becoming nothing more than breeders and caretakers of their children and appendages to their husbands."

"Ouch," grimaced Alice. "But I don't know if I like the sound of words like *infantilized, breeders,* and *appendages* when referring to us. And I don't think I'm filled with rage."

"She interviewed her college classmates," explained Connie, "at a fifteen-year reunion; so these are educated women just like us. And they're complaining that they're defined by their husbands' careers, financial resources, and status. You're so much more than Al, the dentist's wife."

"I think it sounds a bit harsh and extreme, Connie."

"Please read it. I'm giving it to you because you keep saying you should get a job, but you don't. You enlisted in the army in WWII and you were a journalist! At the rate you're going, you'll be a grandmother before you do anything, and then you'll say you have to babysit. You're intelligent and talented. You should be out in the world. Read the book. Please. It will change your life."

"Okay, thank you. I'll take a look at it when I get a chance."

Alice had meant to iron Al's shirts, but it was such a beautiful sunny day that she decided to take the book outside and read on the patio for a bit. She loved days like this, and it would be a treat to admire her rock garden, which was now in full bloom.

She adjusted the chaise lounge and opened the book. Alice's dream had always been to write and publish a book, and she had tried when Marjorie went to kindergarten to write one about her experiences as a WAC in World War II. When the manuscript was finished, she mailed it to a publisher, it was rejected, and she put it aside.

The more she read *The Feminine Mystique,* the more she got the desire to get out of the house and do something meaningful with her life before it was too late. And the angrier she was with herself for not having done something sooner. During the war, working on the military newspaper *Belvoir Castle,* she had felt useful and relevant. But Connie was the only mother on her block of thirty-two families who worked outside the home. And she had only gone back to work full-time a couple of years ago.

When Al returned home that evening, she broached the subject but didn't mention the book. She didn't want him to think she was so easily influenced by Friedan.

"It's a ridiculous idea," Al said. "Do you really want to leave two teenagers unsupervised?"

"They're good kids; they're responsible. I'm not worried that they're going to turn into juvenile delinquents all of a sudden just because I get a job. I'll find something close by."

"And how will you have time for what you normally do every day?"

"What do I do every day? I go shopping, do laundry, and make and plan what we're going to eat for dinner. It fills up my whole day. I bet if I start working, I can do all that after five o'clock."

"I'm not going to stop you from trying," Al said, but Alice could tell by his expression that he was pretty confident no one would hire her. After all, she hadn't worked in many years. "And you know what?" Al said with a magnanimous tone. "If you really want to get out of the house for a few hours, I can find a little job for you in the office. You can answer the phones, make appointments."

Alice bit her tongue. She did not want him to subvert her plan to get a job. The idea of a job was to meet new people, dress and act professionally, and use her skills. Not to do a job in a dental office that anyone without an education or qualifications could do.

When they were both in the army, Alice had felt that they were at least equal. But now, after so many years of being home and trapped in her housewife role, they were no longer equals. Surely Al had repressed the fact that she had held a responsible job and became a sergeant before he did. She had worked with men who respected her intelligence and ability. Hadn't Al married her just because she was smart and interesting and capable? At least, that's what he had said at the time.

But now after so many years of catering to him and being at his beck and call, she feared he saw her in the very role that Betty Friedan had described in her book—a person with no identity of her own, like the TV mothers in the situation comedies such as *Father Knows Best* and *Leave It to Beaver*. With their perfectly coiffed hair, pearls, and aprons over their shirtwaist dresses, they were lovely, mindless accessories to their husbands and solely fulfilled by their marriages, housework, sex lives, and children. To be truly feminine, a woman should not want to work, get an education, or have political opinions.

Alice had to admit that her life was now a far cry from when she was a star student at NYU and then a reporter at Fort Belvoir. She had felt as if she had power then, but now she realized she was powerless in a man's world. During the war, women had assumed men's jobs and performed admirably. But as soon as the war was over, they were expected to be housewives and babymakers. Alice loved her children; indeed, she had always wanted to be a mother. But her children didn't need her home all day anymore while they were in school. And before long, they would be in college, and then what would she do?

Al could be a little pompous, Alice realized. She remembered the big words with the dictionary definitions he had sent her during their post office courtship. And when she thought about their relationship now, she realized that she was pretty much waiting on him hand and foot. She cooked the meals and served the meals and he gave his opinion like a food critic. "This is a little salty," he would say of her special meatloaf recipe. "This tasted better the last time you made it" was one of his favorite expressions. Now she began to think, *Who had anointed him a food critic?* She was determined to get a job. She would stop washing and ironing his shirts herself and send them out. She would stop cooking elaborate recipes and serve him fish sticks, pizza, and hamburgers. Let him learn to get up off his favorite chair and look in the fridge himself to see what was there.

A couple of days later, Connie knocked on the door again. "So did you start reading the book yet?"

"I actually finished it."

"And what did you think?"

"I think I'm ready to go back to work. But I have no idea how to start looking."

"Well, you're in luck. There's an opening in the public relations department at the hospital. The title is secretary, but I'm sure once they realize your talents and background, you'll be running the office." Connie whipped out a piece of paper with a name and phone number. "Here's the number of the personnel office. Call right away."

Alice walked into the personnel office of the local hospital two days later and was immediately sent to the public relations office for an interview. The manager of the office, Elliot

Goldstone, was in his forties, with sandy-colored hair and brown eyes and wearing a dark blue suit with a white shirt and a thin tie. On his desk was what Alice assumed was a photograph of his family—an attractive wife and two school-age kids. The wall was mostly covered with framed newspaper articles, including some cartoons. Marjorie flinched when her eye caught one that appeared to be from *Playboy* magazine. It depicted a man, likely the president of his company, peering down his female secretary's top. Alice looked at the woman in the cartoon taking notes and it was clear that she was uncomfortable with his leering.

Elliot caught her eye and said: "You know, the first qualification for PR is that you need a thick skin and a sense of humor to do this job. Do you have that?"

"Of course," Alice replied as she quickly pulled herself together. She wanted this job, no matter what. If the boss was a lech, she could handle it. She was a married woman with two children, whose family kidded her that she didn't have a sense of humor.

Elliot said he was impressed with her NYU degree and the public relations experience she had as a WAC. But he had some concerns.

"What happens when your children are sick?" he asked.

"My mother will take care of them."

He then described the achievements of the hospital she would be helping promote—a premature baby nursery, a nuclear medicine department, outpatient clinics for epilepsy, cerebral palsy, infertility, and more. And, of course, there were always human interest stories.

She was hired on the spot and went to work the following week. Alice was thrilled with her new position. She learned very quickly that although her title was secretary, Elliot wasn't much of a hard worker. He was a glad-hander, a friendly, smiley guy. Seldom in the office, he spent much of the day going around the hospital making friends and schmoozing, especially with those who were in high places. She soon realized that she would be doing Elliot's job too—looking for stories, writing press releases, interfacing with the media. At first, all this stimulation gave her a heady feeling.

The first major story she shepherded was when a ten-year-old boy, Ronnie Cassidy, arrived at the hospital, bleeding and unconscious. He had been riding his bicycle when a car swerved around a corner, throwing him and his bike in different directions. When the operation was over, the internal bleeding had been stopped, the spleen had been removed, and all broken limbs had been set, but Ronnie was in a coma. Elliot told Alice that if he awakened within forty-eight hours, he might not have brain damage.

The forty-eight hours passed, and Ronnie remained comatose. The newspapers had covered the accident, and Mr. Cassidy had spoken to them right after it happened because he wanted the prayers of the community focused on his son. He welcomed the publicity and now was relieved to have the hospital's PR department handle the media. Elliot handed this first big assignment to Alice, telling her she would be the hospital's press liaison; she was thrilled with the responsibility and the challenge.

On the fourteenth day following the accident, Ronnie's mother collapsed in his hospital room. The unit clerk on the pediatric floor told Alice that Mrs. Cassidy had become hysterical and that her doctor had insisted she go home and sleep.

"There is absolutely nothing you can do here," he said. "The nurses are competent, the doctors are in constant attendance, and if there is a change, we'll call you immediately."

The physician also told Mr. Cassidy that he should return to work. "It will be better for you. There could be no change for weeks."

"I can't work," Mr. Cassidy explained. "Because I talk to Ronnie all day long. I've got to keep trying to make him hear me. I'm not giving up. I'll never give up."

Alice happened to be in the room and asked the father if she might share his words with the media. He agreed and she ran to the typewriter and wrote a press release, quoting Mr. Cassidy's comments. Her headline was "The Ronnie Story," the young boy being cared for by "the Hospital with a Heart." Within minutes, she sent it to not only newspapers, but TV and radio as well. It described how Mr. Cassidy remained at Ronnie's bedside, talking continuously, attempting to pierce his son's subconscious. Elliot was very pleased as he made the rounds in the hospital taking credit for the wonderful coverage of this father and son.

The media narrative that Alice crafted also featured the dedicated nurses and doctors, as well as the entire hospital staff praying for and working for Ronnie's recovery. Reporters wrote about how the resolute father spoke of everything he could recall—of the wonderful weeks they had spent at the beach, of Ronnie's friends and how concerned they were about him, of baseball and football and school and parties.

The interns on the case were interviewed as well as the nurses as they emotionally described the beautiful little ten-year-old. With eyes filled with tears, Mr. Cassidy spoke directly to the cameras: "Please help us," he implored the audience. "We need your help. Please offer prayers for Ronnie. We will be grateful. Please pray for him."

Alice was thrilled by the amazing coverage she had generated for the hospital. And so was Elliot, who took full credit for it. The leadership, and even the board of the hospital, took notice of the amazing work by the PR department, led by Elliot. There was a remarkable response to the TV coverage. Cards, prayers, and religious symbols began arriving at the hospital by the hundreds. Letters offering advice and consolation were delivered.

The hospital higher-ups and even the board took notice of the spectacular media coverage, and Elliot became the man of the hour while Alice was unnoticed. Elliot even had the audacity to put his arm around her and say, "You're doing a great job, honey. PR people are supposed to be invisible."

She continued inviting the media in to view the men and women who came to the hospital to express their concern, some with prayer books, a few kneeled in prayer.

While Alice was proud of herself, she believed this story would not have a good ending. *How could a child recover after being in a coma for so long?*

But then on the sixty-fourth day, the miracle happened.

Mr. Cassidy remembered that Ronnie loved horses. Although they lived in Queens, he had spent the past two summers riding horses in a camp on Long Island.

"Ronnie, listen," Mr. Cassidy implored his son. "Open your eyes. I have an idea. You know how you love horses. I've decided that when you are well, we're going to move to the country and I'm going to buy you your own horse."

He kept repeating those words over and over again. He thought he saw Ronnie's eyelids flutter. He pressed the call button.

The doctors and nurses at his bedside urged him, "Tell it to him again."

He repeated the promise of the home in the country and a horse.

The child's eyes opened slowly and a weak smile appeared on his face.

The entire hospital was jubilant and that afternoon TV cameras were set up.

"The public has helped with their prayers and we wanted to share this joyous event with all of you," Mr. Cassidy said to the cameras.

Newspaper reporters roamed the halls interviewing personnel for their reactions.

Elliot called Alice into his office to thank her for her efforts. "You did a great job, young lady. I, for one, am very appreciative of your part in what we did to put the hospital on the map. I'd like to take you out to lunch, and I'm putting in for a raise for you—$10 a week."

"Thank you," Alice said. But she had seen all too clearly what her role was. The woman behind the scenes: faceless, nameless, making her male boss—a show horse—look good.

In fact, she made him look so good that within a year, he was promoted to director of the hospital. The board loved all the positive public relations. A seasoned male reporter from *Newsday* was hired to head the PR department. Of course, Elliot took Alice with him to the administration wing as his secretary. She remained in that position for the next twenty years, running the hospital in secret.

9

The Cantor Sings

Marjorie and the Amazing Voice

As a member of the search committee for a cantor at the Salk Street Jewish Center, I had interviewed and auditioned countless candidates to find the successor to our cantor, Shlomo Rubinoff, who had decided a year ago to move to Austin, Texas. As the committee chair, it was my job to listen to all the audition tapes we received and invite for an in-person audition those we believed may have the special quality I was looking for.

Like other conservative synagogues, ours depended on an engaging rabbi and a dynamic cantor to fill the pews each Shabbat. Our rabbi was just what we needed, and now we had to make sure the cantor we chose complemented him.

It was not until the beginning of April that the cantor of our dreams materialized. His audition tape had sounded promising, but when he and his wife arrived for the in-person audition, he blew us all away the moment he stepped behind the bima.

His name was Pierre Sarfati, a forty-seven-year-old Frenchman who had dark wavy hair and dreamy eyes to match. He was reputed to have performed at the Opéra Bastille in Paris, and I didn't doubt it. Needless to say, our entire committee was smitten with him and immediately invited him to audition at a Shabbat service two weeks hence.

Word of his phenomenal voice leaked out, and congregants excitedly called each other to make sure they were all coming to hear him. Even Pearl Marcus, who wore ear plugs to shul every Shabbat and holiday to muffle the voices of our last two cantors, was anxious to hear Sarfati's magnificent voice.

About two hundred congregants came to hear him at Friday night services, and another five hundred filled the sanctuary the next morning when he led Shabbat services.

"Now that's a hazzan!" Pearl exclaimed to her husband as she choked back tears the moment Sarfati opened his mouth Shabbat morning.

"He's amazing," my friend Stephanie told me. "He's just what we need."

Pierre was quickly hired.

While the neighboring synagogues shrank, folded, or merged with others, SSJC continued to grow as word spread about Pierre's exceptional talent. People who were three-day-a-year Jews started attending Shabbat mornings or Friday nights to watch and listen; couples who had quit the synagogue after their last child's bar or bat mitzvah rejoined; members of neighboring shuls began migrating.

"It was like a concert, a Broadway show," former sisterhood president Nancy Dubin told me after a Shabbat service. "Can you believe I'm finally a shul-goer?"

As a board member, I was happy that attendance was growing. But I had to concede that Pierre was no Cantor

Rubinoff in the hospitality department. But memories being short, most of the members soon forgot about the Shabbat dinners they enjoyed at the Rubinoffs' home, not to mention his wife's warm smile, delicious raisin challahs, melt-in-your-mouth brisket, and babka that oozed with chocolate.

Rather than inviting congregants to his home, Pierre was swamped with invitations from members to come to their homes for dinner. Who wouldn't want this charismatic cantor to grace their Shabbat table with his charm and voice?

But on the weekend Stephanie invited Pierre and his wife to her home for Shabbat dinner, he didn't bring his wife. Stephanie had invited my husband, Eric, and me, as well as a few other empty nesters. Pierre's talents were on display as he opened with an operatic kiddush and closed with a blessing after the meal worthy of an Oscar.

The following Monday as Stephanie and I took a walk through the gated community into which we had both moved after our children grew up and left home, I said to her, "Your dinner was lovely. You really outdid yourself. But where was the wife?"

"I don't know," said Stephanie. "We haven't seen her since he was hired. The scuttlebutt is that she's an opera singer and has her own busy schedule."

"She looks young enough to be his daughter," I said.

"Well, she's his second wife and they don't have any children. Pierre's first wife is in Paris, and they reportedly have grown children in Israel."

"I have to tell you, Stephanie," I said, "I know everyone is in love with him and his voice, but I think he's in love with himself. It's all a show. I'm getting tired of it. Week after week—you can see he just craves the adoration. And if someone gets up to leave during the service, he gives them the evil eye. People do have to go to the bathroom from time to time. It's all about him. I felt that Cantor Rubinoff was our representative to God. This one, it's like he thinks he's in Carnegie Hall."

Three years passed and Pierre's popularity grew, as did that of the Salk Street Jewish Center, which by now had absorbed yet another local temple. Visitors came from throughout Long Island and the metropolitan area to see SSJC's secret weapon. The rabbi then announced his retirement and a search was initiated for a new one. But, truthfully, the rabbi had become incidental; the shul was all about the cantor.

When the search began, some board members suggested offering Pierre a longer contract—some even argued for a lifetime one. The negotiations dragged on for quite some time. Pierre demanded a salary greater than the rabbi's, the entire summer off, and six weeks scattered throughout the year so that he could perform at other venues. After some minor adjustments, a new contract was finally agreed upon. The lawyers then said that according to the synagogue's constitution, it had to be presented and voted on by the entire congregation.

It was a well-attended congregational meeting with Pierre's many fans giving testimonies to his positive influence on them and their children. Speaker after speaker lauded his talents and professionalism. And then Dr. Martin Breyer, an esteemed surgeon in the community, rose to speak. He was about sixty years old, with gray hair and black horn-rimmed glasses. He wore a suit and tie.

"I do not like to engage in *lashon hara,*" he said. "And it is not my habit to get involved in shul politics. But this cult of the cantor has gotten out of hand. My home is directly across the street from the cantor's residence, and because of my work, I keep odd hours. I will just simply say that in three years I have never seen the cantor's wife, but I have observed countless young women coming and going from that residence at all hours of the day and night."

There was a collective gasp, followed by whispering.

The president turned beet red and banged his gavel.

A heavy blond woman standing in the back started yelling: "He ruined my daughter."

A man with a Mets cap and T-shirt ran to the front and grabbed the microphone. "This is a *shanda*! The whole board should resign."

The lone security guard and some custodians tried to quell the inflamed audience, which suddenly went from wanting to give the cantor a lifetime contract to burning him at the stake.

The president announced the meeting was over. And so was the short and illustrious career of Cantor Pierre Sarfati at the Salk Street Jewish Center.

Years later when people inquired about the demise of the SSJC, how it had so quickly lost its cache, hemorrhaged members, and rented space in the building to a revivalist church before shutting down, the answer we gave was always, "changing demographics."

10

Cherished Daughter

The tradition of a close mother-daughter relationship ran deep in Marjorie Grossman's family.

At thirteen, her grandmother, Sadie, stayed home and helped her mother with the housework and with caring for her six younger siblings in their cramped and dark Hester Street tenement. Sadie was smart and spirited and worked her way through night school. When she secretly applied to nursing school and was accepted, her mother refused to let her go. Dutiful daughter that she was, Sadie obeyed her mother's edict but regretted it the rest of her life.

Marjorie's mother, Alice, was the only child of Sadie and her husband, Mayer, to live to adulthood. One baby boy was stillborn, and their son, Bernie, contracted polio and later died from pneumonia at age eight. Alice lost her father when Marjorie was twelve and insisted that Sadie come and live with her family, fearful of losing her mother too if she were left alone.

Marjorie too had a special bond with her mother. She was her best friend, confidante, and companion. They were on the phone together half a dozen times a day. When something happened at work, Marjorie would pick up the phone and call her mother. When she had an issue with one of her children, Alice would give her sage advice. When she got so angry at her husband that she wanted to divorce him, she would call her mother crying.

"Eric loves you," Alice would say in her soothing voice. "Just ignore him."

Marjorie initially intended to take a few years off to raise her three sons—the twins, Adam and Seth, and their brother, Joshua, who was three years younger. The twins had been a handful, but her mother had been there for her, helping her every step of the way. She would appear at Marjorie's sprawling colonial at eight o'clock in the morning three days a week and let herself in through the back door. Before she even said hello to Marjorie, she would head to the laundry room, put in a load of wash, and then straighten up the kitchen. After she finished her self-assigned chores, she'd head up to the twins' bedroom, where she'd grab one of the crying babies from Marjorie's arms and walk him around with a little bounce, whispering soothing words as she walked.

Marjorie often thought to herself that if she had not had her mother nearby, she would have stopped at the twins. They were cute and sweet but colicky as infants and then very mischievous and active as they got older—fighting with each other, wrestling, throwing balls in the house, and making more than one hole in the wall. When outside, if they saw a puddle on the street, they would rush to splash in it, rather than walking around it. Marjorie's husband, Eric, was an orthopedic surgeon who worked long and irregular hours, causing her to feel like a single mother much of the time.

When the twins were three years old and in nursery school, she gave birth to Josh, a chubby, placid, quiet baby, whom she got to enjoy for the three hours a day the twins were in school. She told herself, "This is my portion in life—to have three healthy sons. Thank you, God. *Baruch HaShem.*"

But once Josh was about two, he became part of the jumping on the couch, the wrestling, the ball throwing, and the puddle splashing. It felt to Marjorie as if Eric was hardly ever home, and when he was, he was exhausted and uncommunicative—and she did everything. When she was thirty-six on a routine visit to her gynecologist, he asked if she wanted to have her tubes tied. The twins were ten years old by then and Josh was seven. She thought about it for a while, but she was not one for elective procedures, and although she was pretty sure she was done, surgery felt just too final to her.

At about the same time, she began to put out feelers about going back to teaching full-time now that Josh was in school all day. She called her former principal, who was now a superintendent of schools in another district, and he said he would keep her in mind and speak to some of his colleagues in other districts. She typed up her resume, made copies, and started shopping for work-appropriate clothing.

Her periods had always been irregular, so it wasn't surprising when she missed a month. But now she had missed two and she was starting to feel bloated and somewhat nauseous.

She called her mother, crying.

"Why are you crying?" her mother asked. "Maybe you'll have a daughter."

"I spoke with Phil Baker and he's going to help me get a teaching job. I have it all planned out: I'll go back to school at night and get a certificate in administration. Then I'll be a principal. Anyway, I'm sure I'll have another son."

"Sons are wonderful. Believe it or not, they're actually easier to raise."

"Are you saying it was easier to raise Barry than me?"

"It was different," her mother explained. "He was the older one and he was more independent. He was a sweet, loving little boy."

"And now? How often does he call?"

"Well, you know. He tries."

"Yeah, I know. Oh, you mean his wife. You really believe Trudy calls the shots. Do you really think it's her fault he hardly ever calls or visits only on holidays and special occasions? New Jersey really isn't that far."

"Well, you know what they say. *A son's a son till he takes a wife, but a daughter's your daughter for all of your life.*"

"Great, so that's what I have to look forward to."

"Not necessarily. You have three sons; hopefully one—if not all—will be there for you in your old age. Just pray they marry nice girls who understand the importance of family."

"Mom, this is ridiculous. They're eight and five. You're jumping ahead way too far."

"I'm just saying, if you are pregnant—which is yet to be determined—you could have a daughter."

"I doubt it."

"You don't know—no one knows."

"What about my career plans?"

"They waited this long; they can wait another few years."

By the time Marjorie went for her ob-gyn appointment, she had talked herself into wanting another child. And Eric was all for it; he loved the idea of four children.

"Why would you want another child?" Marjorie asked him. "So you can tell your patients? You're never around."

"That's not fair," he retorted. "I always wanted a big family. But if you want an abortion, that can easily be arranged."

"I don't think I could handle it. For my whole life, I'd always be thinking of what might have been—what age the baby would be and what he or she would be doing."

"Well, then," Eric said, "in that case, I think we need to embrace the idea of a fourth child."

As Marjorie sat in the waiting room and looked at the pregnant women and the baby magazines, she knew she was going to be very disappointed if she were not pregnant. She dreamed about her little girl; sweet, docile, dressed in pink frills, a daughter for all of her life. And in a year or two, she could start taking administration courses and, if her mother helped her out, she could dip her toes into the school pool by substitute teaching. By the time she was forty-two, the baby would be in school full-time and she could go back to teaching. After she taught for a few years, she would apply for administrative positions.

Since she was past thirty-five, her doctor recommended amniocentesis, a procedure that would tell her the health and sex of the fetus. Marjorie opted not to know. She would find out the moment the baby was born.

"That's crazy," said her mother. "Do you realize that every doctor, nurse, technician, and clerical person who looks at your chart knows what you're having? Don't you want to know?"

"No, I don't, Mom. If I find out it's a boy now, I might feel let down. But at the moment of birth, the only thing that will matter is if the baby is healthy."

Once the due date approached, Marjorie's parents came to stay in the spare bedroom of her sprawling colonial to help with the boys and to be there when their daughter went into labor.

"It's a girl!" Brad Goldstein, the ob-gyn and friend and colleague of Eric's, shouted triumphantly as the baby was born. Eric grasped Marjorie's hand and kissed her forehead and they both wept with joy. They named her Deborah Sharon after Alice's grandmother.

When they brought the baby girl home from the hospital, Marjorie saw that her mother had decorated the house with pink and white balloons and vases of pink and white roses and carnations. When the boys came home from school, everyone crowded into the baby's beige bedroom (it had been painted a neutral color to be safe) and marveled at the sleeping bundle of pink.

"This is your new baby sister, Deborah. You are all her big brothers, and you will teach her many things when she gets older."

"When can we play with her?" Josh wanted to know.

"Not for several months. Right now, she's too young to play with. But you can help me with her."

As Deborah grew, the boys were helpful and treated her like the precious little gift that she was. Marjorie and her mother delighted in dressing her in pink—frilly party dresses, bows in her hair, skirts, tops, pants. But Deborah also had a mind of her own, and once she was old enough, she also favored purple and red. With her dark wavy hair, round face, hazel eyes, and perfect bowlike lips, she only grew more beautiful as the years passed.

Her bat mitzvah was quite the affair, with the twins and Josh coming in from college to share the festive weekend. Deborah wowed the family and the congregation by conducting the entire Shabbat service, the haftarah and Torah reading, save for the three portions chanted by her brothers. Deborah's speech was a huge sensation. Unlike many children her age, she enunciated perfectly. Linking the Torah portion to the present and future, she spoke about how it was up to young people to make the world a better place. Both the rabbi and president of the synagogue went on and on about how special Deborah was and what a fine family she came from. What *nachas*!

The party was a two-day affair, with a catered luncheon after services and then a big party after Shabbat with a six-person band that played endless horas as well as popular music for the two hundred guests. There were also games and entertainment for the fifty best friends of the bat mitzvah girl.

As Deborah moved on from middle to high school, she continued to be an outstanding all-around straight-A student. Under Marjorie's tutelage and with the advice of her big brothers, she easily navigated the teenage social scene, and by the time she was a junior, she was on the high honor roll, an editor of the school newspaper, president of her synagogue youth group, and popular among both boys and girls.

Marjorie had been teaching for a few years now when Phil Baker called her and said,

"Marjorie, there's an opening in the district for an elementary school principal. It's a wonderful school and I think it might be a good fit for you. Let me know if you want to apply."

She discussed it with Eric.

"Sounds like it's right up your alley," he said. "And you enjoy working with Phil. I would definitely go for the interview and see what happens."

"But Deborah's going to be a senior and we have to start looking at colleges," Marjorie responded. "She's nervous already and I'm a wreck. *We* have to write an essay or maybe more than one. All those applications are so daunting, and we have to decide if she's going to apply for early decision. In addition, I need to be available to her if she gets depressed or dejected—or worse still, rejected."

"So you're going to forgo your own career plans because our daughter is going to college?" Eric asked. "Just put them on hold? That's counterintuitive. She's going away to college. Do you think she's going to call you half a dozen times a day and ask your opinion about everything?"

"Why not?"

"First, because college is supposed to be a time when young people learn some independence. Second, this is a great opportunity for you. Phil called you himself. He's in a top district. That might not happen again. And weren't you able to juggle everything when the boys went to college? I don't remember you devoting yourself 24/7 to their college selection process, or that they called you—even once a week—when they went away to college. And they all turned out just fine."

"But there's a mysterious, magical bond between a daughter and a mother, Eric. You don't understand because you're a male. She needs me. I've been with her every step of the way; I'm not going to abandon her now and take on the burden of a new and demanding job."

Eric twisted his mouth and shrugged his shoulders.

And when she told Eric that Deborah wanted to look at ten colleges, he was incredulous:

"Are you kidding me? I don't care about all those application fees, but do you really intend to visit all of them? Just so you know, I'm not going to be able to get away to look at so many schools."

That was fine with Marjorie. She would have her daughter all to herself. They drove all over the Eastern Seaboard together, looking at colleges—Boston University, Tufts, Brandeis, Brown, University of Massachusetts, University of Pennsylvania, Penn State, George Washington, NYU, Cornell. They stayed at hotels and bed-and-breakfasts and ate together in restaurants. They finished each other's sentences. *A wonderful bonding experience of a lifetime,* Marjorie thought. Her own mother was gone now, but her daughter was her best friend. Her sons were wonderful, but she was so thankful she had a girl who would take care of her in her old age.

Deborah graduated from the University of Pennsylvania magna cum laude and enrolled at Columbia Law School in the fall later that year. Three years later, she was the class speaker at graduation. Marjorie and Eric kvelled to see their beautiful, intelligent, and well-spoken daughter at center stage. And they were excited to meet a young man Deborah had met in law school, Todd Katzman, a nice Jewish boy from New Jersey, whom Deborah had been dating for the past three months.

Six months after graduation, they became engaged. Marjorie planned every detail of Deborah's extravagant wedding. The couple—both practicing lawyers—had jobs at top law firms in New York City and they rented an apartment on the Upper East Side.

Three years later Deborah was pregnant but wanted to continue her career after she had the baby. So Marjorie thought it would be a fitting time to retire in order to help her. It was something several of her friends were doing for their grandchildren. Marjorie had helped with her six other grandchildren as much as her sons' wives wanted and would allow. But this was her daughter's child! Surely, she could be as close to this grandchild as her own mother had been to Deborah.

Six weeks after Jessica was born, Deborah returned to work. That morning, Marjorie awakened in her Melville home at 5:30 a.m., agonizing about what was going on in Deborah's apartment and how difficult it must be for her to have to leave her tiny baby with a stranger. Three hours later, she was dressed and worrying about the competence of the new babysitter. Alone in her house, she became so obsessed over this that she decided that she had to check for herself.

She got into her car and headed first to the bagel store to buy bagels, cream cheese, lox, and tuna fish for lunch. Then she decided to stop at the kosher butcher and bought two rotisserie chickens, coleslaw, and potato salad for Deborah and Todd's dinner. She then took the Long Island Expressway west toward the city. As she approached the Fifty-Ninth Street Bridge, the traffic slowed, but she made the whole trip from Suffolk County in an hour and a half.

While her husband always made a game of finding a parking space in Manhattan, Marjorie would have none of that. They could well afford a garage. She pulled into one across the street from Deborah's apartment and walked into the beautiful building, which had a large gym and swimming pool.

The doorman greeted her and called up to announce her arrival. He put his hand over the receiver and said to Marjorie: "She says she's not expecting visitors and that Mrs. Grossman-Katzman gave her explicit instructions not to open the door for anyone."

"Who says? I'm her mother, I'm the grandmother. I brought all this food."

"The babysitter. You can leave the food with me," said the doorman.

"I'm sure this is a misunderstanding," Marjorie said. "I'll call my daughter."

She went outside and dialed her daughter's cell. No answer. The voicemail came on, but Marjorie was now shaking and too upset to leave a message.

Now in a state of panic, she called Deborah's office.

"She's in a meeting with a client," said her secretary, Nancy.

"Nancy, her babysitter won't let me into the apartment. I just want to check on the baby, and I brought some food for Deborah and Todd."

"She gave me explicit instructions not to interrupt her, but the meeting should be over in about fifteen minutes, Mrs. Grossman, so I'll be sure to give her your message then."

Marjorie wanted to scream and cry, but what could she do? "Okay, thanks," she said.

She then called Josh, who picked up his cell phone immediately. He was a hospital administrator and worked nearby. By now she was sobbing.

"What's the matter, Mom? I can't understand you. Where are you?"

"I'm in front of Deborah's building. The babysitter won't let me in."

"You're kidding."

"Why would I kid about that?" She continued sobbing.

"I have an hour until my next meeting," Josh said. "Meet me at Starbucks. There's one across the street."

Shlepping the shopping bags of food, Marjorie crossed the street. Her face was red and bloated and streaked with tears.

As Josh walked toward her, she noticed that he looked so handsome and professional in his sports jacket.

He gave her a big hug and she sobbed some more.

"Let's go in," he said. "Go sit down at that empty table in the corner and I'll get us some coffee."

Marjorie sat down at the table and Josh returned with two coffees.

"So, what the hell is going on?" he asked as he set the two cups of coffee on the small table and sat down.

"Deborah's babysitter won't let me in the apartment. She told the doorman that she had instructions not to let anyone in. I get that. But I'm her mother. If this woman is so stupid to not understand that I'm Deborah's mother and her best friend, I'm not so sure I trust her with Jessica."

"You know, Mom, you've always given Deborah a pass. I don't know if it's because she's a girl or your fourth child, but you've always been much harder on the rest of us. Tell me that you never noticed that she can be a bitch."

"Why do you say that, Josh?"

"Because it's true. She was given everything on a silver platter. We all doted on her and everything has to be her way."

"Isn't that a little harsh? She's still postpartum and it's her first day back at work. I really think it's too soon."

"Perhaps, but you noticed I picked up the phone when you called. And you know Joanie and the kids love you so much. You're always welcome in our home. But I don't recall that you ever just dropped in without first letting us know."

"I wouldn't do that to a daughter-in-law."

"Well, I think it's always a good idea to call ahead, Deborah's no exception. Can I ask why you didn't?"

"I just always felt like we were joined at the hip. That we could read each other's minds. That she would appreciate a gesture like that."

"Well, maybe she does," said Josh. "But in the future, I would call first."

Marjorie's cell phone rang. It was Deborah on the line.

"Mom, what were you thinking—showing up with no notice? The babysitter has Jessica on a strict schedule and she was just following instructions. Anyway, she's sleeping now. If you want to go in and take a peek, go ahead. And in the future, check with me first. Okay?"

"Sure," Marjorie said.

"I'm going back to work. This is crazy and it's my first day back."

"Okay."

"Bye, Mom."

Marjorie started sobbing again.

"She said I can take a peek at the baby, but that's it," she told Josh.

"So what did you want?"

"Well, if I had any principles, I would just leave. But how can I resist even a glimpse of my granddaughter?"

"Okay, let's go. I'm coming with you," said Josh.

"Don't you have to go back to work?"

"After we do this."

Josh took the shopping bags and walked across the street with his mother.

When they entered the building, the doorman gave them a sheepish smile. "The missus called and cleared up the misunderstanding, ma'am. I'm sorry."

"No problem," said Josh.

They took the elevator up to the sixth floor, and when they got there, the babysitter, a young woman who looked to be in her twenties, came to the door and introduced herself as Kim. Her hair was in a ponytail and she wore jeans and a T-shirt. Marjorie had expected an old battle-axe of a person—officious, stern, and bossy. It was clear, much to her chagrin, that this young thing had just been following instructions. *But you'd think Deborah might have told her ahead of time to make an exception for her mother! I guess she didn't think it was important to mention that she had a special relationship with me.*

"I'm Josh, Deborah's brother, and this is our mother, Marjorie. She brought you some food for lunch, and dinner for the baby's parents."

"Oh, that's so nice, thank you," Kim gushed.

"Deborah said we can take a peek at the baby," said Josh.

"Of course," Kim said as she led them into the baby's room, a confection of pink and purple.

Marjorie gazed at the sleeping bundle, so sweet, innocent, and precious, and she wondered, *What kind of daughter and granddaughter would she grow up to be?*

As she drove home on the Long Island Expressway, she listened to music of the eighties—the decade in which Deborah was born. It usually comforted her, but now it made her heart break.

She had given her daughter everything it was in her power to give. Much more than she had ever been given. Not just material things, but her attention, her aspirations, her company, her heart.

After what she had just experienced, she was no longer certain that Deborah would be the child who would be there for her in her old age—as she had been there for her mother, and her mother had been there for her grandmother. Now it was crystal clear that Deborah Sharon Grossman-Katzman was the child of a new generation—one of entitlement and empowerment and privilege.

Marjorie wondered if it was too late to purchase long-term care insurance.

11

"I Could Have Written That Book"

Marjorie parked her gray Lexus in the synagogue parking lot. She was about fifteen minutes early for the semiannual book and author event, but she was surprised to see that there were only eight other cars in the parking lot. She snickered to herself that perhaps her longtime friend and former colleague Cynthia Levy was not the big success she imagined herself to be. Marjorie checked herself in the car mirror, reapplied lipstick, and stepped out of the car, her hair freshly blown, wearing a black pantsuit with a red shell. She clutched a copy of Cynthia's newest novel, *Friends We Keep,* which she had purchased on Amazon. Although she had finished the book three months ago, she had not yet written a review as Cynthia had implored her to do. Cynthia had explained that if she could get fifty reviews or more, according to Amazon's mysterious algorithms, it would help her sales. But the only thing Marjorie could think of to write was *I could have written this book myself.*

As she entered the synagogue lobby she spotted Bobbi Shapiro, who had also taught elementary school with her and Cynthia. Bobbi was a perpetually cheerful brunette with short, naturally curly hair, who was always trying to lose ten pounds. She still credited Hillary Clinton for giving her the courage to eschew skirts; Bobbi wore pantsuits for synagogue and cocktail parties. The defining moment was when in 2000, Hillary appeared at the Village School, where they taught, to celebrate the publication of her book, *It Takes a Village*. The then First Lady wore a red pantsuit and white top, and Bobbi later displayed the photo of the two of them taken that day on her fireplace in which they both wore red pantsuits. Today, she looked neat in a pair of black pants and a teal sweater with matching turquoise jewelry.

Bobbi was also holding a copy of Cynthia's book for her to sign and greeted Marjorie with a big smile. "Isn't this exciting? Did you see Cynthia on News 12 last week talking about her book? I bet her former students were as excited as we were!"

Marjorie grudgingly smiled.

"The amazing thing is that she was able to base her novel on so many of the situations we experienced as teachers," Bobbi continued. "It's a real insider's perspective and she raises so many important educational issues. She really nailed the superintendent, don't you think? Clever that she made the character a woman instead of a man. She's so talented!"

Marjorie forced another smile, but she couldn't help how she felt. It could all be boiled down to one sentence: I *could have written that book*.

Marjorie and Bobbi entered the ballroom where there were about twelve round tables with blue tablecloths set up.

There were blue and white carnations in white plastic vases. There was a group of six women huddled around Cynthia.

"We should go say hello," Bobbi said as she began to walk in Cynthia's direction. Marjorie followed. They caught Cynthia's eye and she excused herself from the admiring gaggle and gave each of the women a big hug.

"Thanks so much for coming. I can't tell you how much it means to me to have you both here. I'm a little nervous; I understand there are 120 people registered for the event."

"You'll be great," Bobbi said.

"Yes, of course you will," added Marjorie.

"Get some coffee and a bagel and find a good seat. There's a Q & A at the end and I might need you to ask a question or two to get the ball rolling."

The two women took seats at a table where there were some other teachers from their school.

"Isn't this exciting?" a short, stocky woman with gray hair and blue nail polish exclaimed.

"Cynthia is a genius," said Bonnie, a fifth-grade teacher. "I wonder if Jeb has read it yet and figured out the woman superintendent is really him."

"Unlikely," said Marjorie. "I doubt that he even reads."

"No, he does. He told me he's a big fan of Jodi Picoult. Anyway, Dan Ellis from the local paper did a big spread on Cynthia. Neither Jeb nor the board members could miss it."

By eleven o'clock, all the seats had been taken and the program began.

Anna Klein, the president of the synagogue, introduced Marci Geller, a retired librarian, who was tasked with introducing Cynthia and interviewing her.

As she listened to Marci speak, Marjorie noted that Cynthia's resume was very similar to hers—BA from

Queens College, MA from Hofstra, teacher for twenty-six years; married, mother, grandmother—except for one part: "and in her retirement, she carved out a new career as an author."

"We're so proud of our homegrown author, Cynthia Levy, who I'm going to interview today about her fourth book, *Friends We Keep*. With all the emphasis and concern about our educational system, Cynthia's book raises important issues. The fact that she did this through fiction makes it even more relatable and colorful.

"When did you start writing?"

"I've been writing since the third grade when my story about a snowman with a heart was published in the school newspaper. But I didn't tackle writing a book until I retired."

"Tell us about your writing process."

"After I have breakfast and coffee, I walk for an hour and ideas percolate. Then I sit at my desk and write until lunchtime."

"What was the inspiration for *Friends We Keep*?"

"Well, of course, it's fictional, but I wanted to address some of the issues that I experienced and are present in all schools."

"How did you choose the title?"

"I didn't." Cynthia laughed. "I had about ten other titles the publisher rejected. This was her choice."

"What message did you want to send to readers?"

"That there are issues that even plague the school districts with stellar reputations. Parents need to be involved and vigilant."

"Who is your favorite character?"

"Oh, it's like asking me who my favorite child is. But if I had to choose it would be Greta, the assistant principal."

"How did your experience as a teacher influence your writing?"

"They say you have to write about what you know. Twenty-six years in the educational system gave me a lot of knowledge about it."

"What's next for Cynthia Levy?"

"I'm thinking of writing a sequel."

Marjorie had to admit that Cynthia was glib. The answers rolled off her tongue seamlessly and she was very animated, smiling and gesturing with her hands. She was attractive and convincing as an author. Cynthia explained that after having worked in schools for so many years, she wanted to address certain issues and thought the best way to do it was through fiction. She had written a few short stories over the years, but not a novel. Once she retired, she joined a couple of book clubs and read two novels a month.

"I needed to unlock the secret of novel-writing," Cynthia said. "So I read books about how to craft a novel and I enrolled in an MFA program. I also joined a writer's workshop, where I shared my story with others, and they critiqued it."

"What's the most gratifying part of your experience as an author?"

"Well, I'd have to say after completing the book and seeing the finished product, it's the support I get from my longtime friends. For example, I'm so touched that several of my colleagues are here, especially my longtime pal, Marjorie."

Marjorie felt her face turning red as she forced herself to smile. She felt so guilty, yet she couldn't control her feelings. Cynthia had been her friend since college. They had double-dated and planned their weddings together, which took place within the same year. Their children were all around the same age.

But Marjorie had been the superior student; while they both had majored in education, Marjorie had been an English minor. Cynthia had merely taken the required English courses and, if Marjorie remembered correctly, hadn't done that well. She remembered how Cynthia had cried to her when she got a D on her paper about *Heart of Darkness* by Joseph Conrad in her freshman year at Queens College. The teacher had written all over it in red that she had not understood the meaning of the book. Now everyone was fawning over Cynthia as if she were a celebrity. It made Marjorie nauseous. *I could be up there,* she thought to herself.

And yet she was ashamed that she had these feelings because Cynthia was not only a good friend but a nice person, the kind of friend who brought chicken soup when you were sick and babysat for your kids when you were in a pinch.

Later that night when she was in bed with her husband, Eric, he said, "What's the matter with you? You've been in a grouchy mood since I got home. Didn't you have a nice time at Cynthia's book event?"

Marjorie choked back the tears and then began sobbing.

He took her hand. "Did I say something wrong? What happened?"

"Nothing happened. I know I shouldn't feel this way. Cynthia has been a good friend, but I know I'm smarter than she is. Everyone thinks she's such a brilliant author."

"I thought you told me her book resonated with you."

"It did; that's just the point. I could have written it. She based so much of the book on what we experienced, what happened to us as teachers."

"But she wrote it," he said. "Plenty of people have the capacity to do things that they don't do. What's the old canard? It's five percent inspiration and ninety-five percent perspiration. She's an old friend, and she's been a good friend. It doesn't make sense to resent her because she did the hard work. And it's admirable that she's reinvented herself."

Marjorie continued to sob. She had made her bed and now she was sleeping in it. She had married a man who didn't have a jealous bone in his body. If you spit in his face, he would tell you it was raining. Marjorie's mother had said to her early on in their marriage, "Eric is a satisfied man." Even though her mother was long gone, Marjorie often remembered her words. It was mind-boggling to her and she was very lucky, she thought, that he was a satisfied man. Marjorie hated this side of herself. She wished she could be happy for Cynthia. She knew that she should write that Amazon review, but the words *I could have written that book* continued to ring in her ears.

The next morning Marjorie woke up knowing that she should call Cynthia and tell her what a great job she did at the book and author luncheon, but she kept stalling. As Marjorie was folding her second load of laundry, her cell phone rang, and she saw that Cynthia was on the phone. She considered not picking it up but then decided that she should.

As soon as she heard Cynthia's voice, she chirped: "You did a great job yesterday. And what a wonderful turnout. It was fun seeing some of our former colleagues."

"Thanks so much, Marjorie. Yes, it was. So, I got an intriguing call this morning. They're setting up a statewide commission on education and they asked me to be on it."

Marjorie rolled her eyes.

"But I really can't take on another commitment. I'm just so busy with the book, I don't have time to attend regular meetings. I said I'd be happy to serve on the advisory committee, but I recommended you for the actual commission. I told them you're not only an outstanding educator, but a great intellect."

"You said that?"

"Yes, of course. I didn't forget that you had toyed with running for school board after we retired. And remember when they tried to recruit you to run for county legislature? You can still do it, you know."

"My mother always said I didn't have a thick enough skin for politics."

"You're more mature now. Anyway, will you do it? I have to get back to the governor's office and let them know."

"Sure." Marjorie was choked up. "Wow, thanks, Cynthia. That's so kind and generous of you."

"You're a good friend and you understand the issues better than anyone. Expect them to contact you soon."

Marjorie left the remaining towels on her bed; she would finish them later. She had to go for a walk and clear her head. She felt a mix of elation and shame. No, there was something she had to do before she went out.

She sat down on her bed with her laptop and went to the *Friends We Keep* page on Amazon. She clicked on "Write a Customer Review." First, she gave the book five stars and the headline "A Compelling and Courageous Novel."

She wrote: *Cynthia Levy has done an amazing job articulating the urgent issues facing students, teachers, and parents today. Through an engaging story and compelling characters, she has brought to life and given voice to the overwhelming needs and challenges, which need to be addressed. As a venerable educator and a talented writer, she had the courage and discipline to write this important novel.*

Marjorie submitted the review, and her conscience was temporarily assuaged. She laced her sneakers, grabbed her cell phone, and headed for the door. It was a sunny spring day, and cherry blossoms were blooming throughout the neighborhood.

12

The End of Giggling

Marjorie's Complicated Memories

When third grade began in the fall, I was certain that the highlight of the year would be Aunt Judy's wedding. I had been looking forward to it as long as I could remember. Aunt Judy was my father's baby sister—she was seventeen years younger than he was, and the youngest of five siblings. I idolized her. She lived with her parents on the Jersey Shore and was always so nice to me when we visited. She took me to the boardwalk where we played Skee-Ball and ate frozen custard cones and saltwater taffy.

My earliest memories were of my mother tucking me into bed and me not wanting to go to sleep. "Think of Aunt Judy's wedding," she said. Invariably, I drifted off to sleep dreaming of white lace bridal gowns, handsome grooms, and me—scattering petals as I walked down the aisle.

When Aunt Judy finally got engaged when I was eight, she brought her fiancé to our home in Queens to meet us. He was dark and handsome and I thought he looked like Elvis.

"We want you to be our flower girl," Aunt Judy told me. "The wedding will be on New Year's Eve."

My mother took me shopping at the May Department Store in a special section where they had beautiful dresses and gowns for girls like me. We settled on a long pink gown that was satin and lace with little pink rosettes. I couldn't wait to show my friends and to wear it. Aunt Judy said that I would have a basket with petals that I would scatter as I walked down the aisle right before she marched down with my grandparents.

Of course, on the way to pick up Grandma Sadie and Grandpa Mayer, my maternal grandparents who were also invited, I threw up in the car. Thankfully, we had decided to change when we got to the hotel. I think it was the excitement, although my mother was worried that perhaps I had another stomach virus. My mother made sure to clean the car when we got to my grandparents' apartment, and my brother, Barry, and I sat in the back with my grandparents on the drive to the hotel.

I made a miraculous recovery by the time we arrived. I remember being in the bridal room with my Aunt Judy and her bridesmaids, who looked so old and grown-up to me. I was a little disappointed that they didn't pay much attention to me.

I always liked to be the center of attention, and for a brief moment as I scattered white petals from my white basket, I was. But then I was relegated to the children's table with my brother and a bunch of other little boys, and my moment in the spotlight was over. After the wedding, my mother said that we should probably have gotten a short dress, like my friend Denise had for her aunt's wedding. It was white organdy with little umbrellas all over it. She got a lot of wear out of it, while I only wore my flower girl gown once.

When I was eight, my social life consisted of calling for my friends on the block. I would ring their doorbells and ask the mothers who opened the doors if their daughters could come out and play. Usually, the answer was in the affirmative. Except for my friend Denise, who sometimes couldn't come out because she was being punished. I couldn't quite understand why she was disciplined so often because my mother never punished me.

If the boys were playing in the street, we would join them in games like Red Light, Green Light and Ringolevio. Other than worrying about the Russians crashing an atomic bomb into our classroom while we crouched under our desks, it was a happy childhood.

When I was eight, I was a giggler. My giggling could be set off by a funny word or thought or by my father tickling my feet. Although I was a good and obedient student, sometimes I could not help myself. Someone would say something that tickled me and off I would go on a giggling fit. Denise was a giggler too, and on one occasion we were both sent to the principal's office for a giggling fit.

My giggling stopped, however, in the spring of third grade.

It happened when Mrs. Baker was our teacher. Mrs. Baker was jolly and motherly and used to tell us about her family. She would bring in the *Long Island Press* and show us her son's name. He was the star football player on his high school team. I remember thinking how important it was to have your name in the newspaper. My name had actually been in the newspaper when Aunt Judy got married. There was a big article about her wedding in the *Asbury Park Press*, and it mentioned everyone in the wedding party, including the flower girl—me, Marjorie.

Back in the 1950s, the classes in our school were homogeneous—and we were in 3-1, the smartest class out of six in the grade. PS 251 was a three-story brick building built in 1928, and the third-grade classes were on the first floor. Due to the baby boom, there were thirty-six kids packed into our classroom. When some of the boys acted up, the teacher wrote a list on the blackboard under the heading *TLBL* with their names under it. It meant *Tentative Left Back List,* and all kids were terrified of being held back and not moving to the next grade with the other students. But my mother told me that none of the kids in 3-1 would ever be left back. Still, it was a good disciplinary device to scare us.

When you're in with other bright kids, you have no idea that you're anything special because you all have similar IQs. The only exception was for spelling; for that subject Mrs. Baker divided us into two groups—albeit very unequal. Thirty-one students were in the white group, and five of us were in the red group. The red group got the harder words. I was a great speller and so were my friends, Ellen and Maureen, and two boys, Peter and Robert. Ellen, Maureen, and I really wanted to be in the white group with the rest of our friends because that's where most of the kids were—including all the popular girls like Denise. But Mrs. Baker said we had to be in the red group.

Ellen was a sweet-faced, chunky, and serious girl. Her father was a pediatrician who saw patients in his home office. But he wasn't my doctor. My mother always took me to Dr. Krinsky, who had an office in a building on Union Turnpike. I didn't like him much. He was a little funny-looking man with dark eyes and a pointy nose. His dark hair was thinning. He didn't talk to me, directing everything at my mother. I associated him with penicillin shots in my rear end. I was certain that he enjoyed hurting kids. That's because every time I was sick and he paid a home visit, he gave me a shot.

In those days, doctors would come to the house if you were sick. Whenever Dr. Krinsky came, he threatened that if I got one more case of tonsillitis, I would have to have my tonsils removed. Even though my friends told me you could eat a lot of ice cream after the operation, it scared me. As soon as my mother called the doctor, I started to worry. I dreaded his visits and the shot.

"Is he going to give me a shot?" I cried each time my mother called the doctor.

"We'll see," she said. But we both knew what "we'll see" meant. And giving shots was a knee-jerk reaction for the doctor. It seemed that the only thing he had in his black bag was an instrument with which to hurt kids.

Each time I heard him ring the bell, I would cringe and pull the blanket over my head. My mother ushered him into the nine-by-twelve-foot bedroom I shared with my brother. She told me to come out from under the covers and show my face. I saw his unsmiling face, very businesslike, holding his black bag, and talking to my mother. Then he'd look in my throat, threaten me with a tonsillectomy, and jab me in the behind.

One day in the winter in the third grade, I had my usual sore throat and fever and Dr. Krinsky was not available. My mother told me that Dr. Rosenbaum, Ellen's father, was coming instead of Dr. Krinsky. At the sound of the doorbell, I panicked. But the minute I saw him, I relaxed. He looked like a cuddly Jewish Santa Claus, without the red costume, of course; he wore a business suit and tie and carried a black medical bag. He had dark brown hair and black horn-rimmed glasses. He smiled at me and in a jolly voice said, "So what's the problem today, princess? You're not feeling so good? I've come to make you better." Then he told my mother and me a few jokes before he looked in my throat.

Much to my delight, he did not jab me in the backside. Instead, he took out his prescription pad and wrote a script for a pink liquid medication, which he told my mother I should take three times a day. And not a word about taking my tonsils out.

"She'll feel better in twenty-four hours, but keep her out of school for three days, then she can go back."

"Goodbye, sweetheart," he said with a big grin as he departed from my room.

I was smitten.

When I returned to Mrs. Baker's class, I felt a new bond with Ellen, the daughter of the very kind and gentle doctor.

About two months later, Ellen was absent from school. Mrs. Baker announced to the class that Ellen's father had died suddenly and we were going to make her sympathy cards. I chose a yellow piece of construction paper and drew a picture of her father, his black bag, and a bottle of medicine. Inside I wrote: "Your father was the best doctor I ever met. His smile and his kindness I will never forget." Mrs. Baker said that what I wrote was very nice and that I should add at the end, "With sympathy to you and your family."

I was shaken by the death of Dr. Rosenbaum, but I didn't talk about it with anyone except my friend Denise, who somehow knew everything. She said Ellen's father had just dropped dead from a heart attack while he was shoveling snow. Now I knew that fathers of third graders could die, and this was very frightening to me. Ellen came back to school for a month or so and then she stopped coming. Mrs. Baker announced to the class that she, her mother, and her sister were moving to New Jersey to be near her grandparents.

Now there were only four students in the red spelling group.

Spring came and the crocuses and tulips started blooming. My mother ordered seeds from the PS 251 fundraiser. I didn't care to get my hands dirty, but my mother took great pride in her little garden in our backyard. Spring vacation came, and we were off from school. My family observed Passover by not eating bread and cake and other things that contained leavening agents. We went to our family Seder.

Passover coincided with Easter that year and my Christian friends, including Denise and Maureen, sported new coats and bonnets. I thought Maureen's coat was beautiful and I wished I had one like hers. It was turquoise, setting off her golden-blond hair and big blue eyes. It had a white collar with sparkling rhinestones.

During the vacation week, I went to Maureen's backyard and we played with the two bunny rabbits and six chicks her father had bought for the Easter holiday. She offered me a chunk of her chocolate bunny rabbit, but I said no thanks because it wasn't kosher for Passover.

About two weeks after we came back to school, Maureen was absent. Maureen was never absent. After school that afternoon when we were playing in Denise's backyard, she told me that Maureen's father had died suddenly. "Probably from a heart attack, like Dr. Rosenbaum," she said.

When I went home I asked my mother, and she confirmed it.

In class we made cards for Maureen, and then she came back to school a few days later and we all told her how sorry we were about her father.

A week later, Mrs. Baker reminded us that a month ago she had asked us to bring in empty coffee cans for a project. She had now lined up all the cans on a back table. I don't remember what the project was; it might have been a science experiment. Maureen asked the teacher if she could take one of the coffee cans home with her and she said yes. I believed that this was a special favor because Maureen had just lost her father.

Now I knew that two of my friends' fathers had died within a few months of each other. I didn't know what to think.

A week later Maureen was absent again.

When I went home I told my mother, and she said Maureen's mother had died.

It was one thing to lose a father, but I thought I couldn't go on living without my mother. I was beside myself. My mother said not to worry, she was very healthy and had no intention of dying.

I was still worried.

"What did she die from?" I asked.

"I don't know," my mother said. "She probably had a disease and was sick for a long time."

But that's not what Denise told me the next day at school. She said Maureen's mother had hanged herself in the basement.

I didn't believe her, but Denise said it was in the newspaper. I figured if it was in the newspaper, it must be true. But as I got older, I began to wonder just why it was a news story worthy of the *New York Post*.

I never saw Maureen again. Mrs. Baker told us she was going to live with her aunt and uncle in East Meadow. I wondered whether they would adopt her, and if she would change her last name. The teacher encouraged us to write to her. I wrote to her, but she didn't answer.

When it came time to choose a representative from our class for the school spelling bee, Mrs. Baker drafted me. I was the last girl still in the red group.

I suppose I was the best speller left in the group. My spelling prowess was abetted by the game I played with my grandfather each week. He would give my brother and me a list of hard words the week before, then ask us to spell them the following week. For every correct answer, we got a nickel or a dime.

I didn't want to be the class representative in the spelling bee. I kept thinking about Ellen and Maureen, Dr. Rosenbaum, and Maureen's parents. Why had they died? Would my parents die too? Did Maureen's mother really hang herself in the basement? If so, why? Maybe Maureen or Ellen would have been better representatives of our class.

But I was a compliant child, so I did what I was told.

My parents and grandparents were excited. They had visions of me competing in the National Spelling Bee. I proceeded to study for the event and my grandfather drilled me. Everyone thought I was well prepared.

On the day of the school spelling bee, the first word I had to spell was *abysmal*. This was a word I had heard in relation to Maureen's parents, but I had not studied how to spell it.

We had to say the word and then spell it.

"Abysmal," said the moderator.

"Abysmal," I repeated as I sounded it out. "A-B-I-S-M-A-L," I said.

"Incorrect," said the moderator.

I was out.

I was shocked. *What did I do wrong?*

When my mother told me later that the word had a *y* in it instead of an *i,* I felt like a failure that I did not know how to spell that word.

"I don't know that word," I said. "What does it mean?"

"It means awful, dreadful, appalling, horrible, very bad," my mother said.

I thought to myself that *abysmal* pretty much described third grade after Aunt Judy's wedding. It would be a word that I would never forget how to spell.

13

Try to Remember

Marjorie and the Impossible Dream

I met Rick in the university bookstore on the first day of school. He said, "Come back to my room, I'll sell you my books for less." I thought that perhaps I shouldn't go back to the room of a complete stranger, but he was in the same graduate program, and he lived in the school's housing, so I decided it was safe. I sat on his single bed in his sparse room while he went about gathering the books. He told me about the classes; he was a year ahead of me, but he was also enrolled in a historiography class I had signed up for. He was very smiley and friendly. He put the books in a neat pile and added up how much I owed him. Although he had highlighted many things in yellow, the cost was considerably less than I would have paid at the bookstore, and I thought I might learn something from the words he had emphasized.

One thing bothered me. He calculated the costs twice and on the second time, he realized it was actually a dollar more than he had first said. I didn't feel like arguing about a dollar, and here I had met a boy on my first day in the program. So I paid him for the books and took them back to my apartment, which I shared with two other girls.

In the class Rick and I had together, the assignment was to research a particular person in a particular year. My person was Henry Morgenthau in 1942. His was Theodore Roosevelt in 1906. I was walking through the stacks looking for information on my person and I saw him at a desk with a pile of books. He gave me a big smile like he was so happy to see me. He said, "Let's go for coffee." So we did.

In addition to the class we were in together, I kept running into him everywhere. He was ubiquitous. Always in the library, at the Vietnam War protest, in the cafeteria, at the mixers, at the lecture when Mark Rudd came to speak, at the Friday night Shabbat dinner. You could say we had similar interests.

At first I wasn't sure he was Jewish because he was dark and swarthy, and he might have been an Arab. But he showed me the watch he got for his bar mitzvah. That didn't mean much to my grandmother when she met him. She had to excuse herself and went to her room to take a pressure pill, my mother told me later. I think it was his long black hair, beard, and mustache that set her off.

I mentioned in passing that I wrote poetry. He said, "Show me your poems." We went to the quad and sat down on a blanket, and he shared that he loved the smell of freshly cut grass. *What a sensitive guy*, I thought. I read him a couple of my poems, which I had only shared with my mother up to then. He looked at me with his big smile while I was reading to him, and he applauded when I finished.

My friend Naomi said she saw us there and she said she could tell he was smitten.

He asked me if I liked the ballet. I said my mother never got around to taking me, but I had always wanted to go. He took me to the ballet and told me what a privilege it was to watch Edward Villella perform. He explained terms to me like *plié* and *pirouette*.

We went bike riding in Central Park. We went to a Pete Seeger concert. He kissed me. He said, "It's too bad we both have roommates."

"Why don't you get your own apartment?" he asked me.

I tingled with the implication that he wanted to make love to me. I figured he couldn't afford his own apartment but didn't understand why he thought I could.

That May he graduated from the program and mysteriously decided to join the Peace Corps. I thought it was to get out of the war, but he could have just taught in the city back then. He went off to Ghana. He wrote to me about once a month. He told me he had to eat bugs because they had trained the volunteers to be respectful of the host country's customs. I lived for those letters.

I wrote back and couldn't decide whether I should sign them *love* or not, because he didn't. I scoured the thesaurus for synonyms, such as *affectionately,* which I settled on. Naomi had some parties, and I met some other boys who asked me out. One of them was a law student whom I dated for several months. He had an apartment in Brooklyn, and he wanted to sleep with me. But I was saving myself for Rick.

I went out with an accountant, who I thought was boring because he didn't care about politics. A boy named Adam in one of my classes followed me around like a puppy dog and I went to the movies with him a few times. Some of my friends were doing Operation Match, but I wasn't going to be matched up by a computer when I had already met the man of my dreams. Every time I saw one of those thin, blue aerogrammes, my heart stopped. I began to count the days until Rick would return.

Sometime after his second year in Ghana, the letters became more sporadic, and in the last few months they stopped entirely. *Had he met a girl?* I wondered. There could have been a female Peace Corps worker that he found attractive and bonded with—or even, perhaps, a Ghanaian. He had written that the Ghanaian people were warm, friendly, and hospitable. He was so liberal and such a bon vivant, it was possible.

He never contacted me again.

Over the years I thought about him, especially when I heard the song "Try to Remember," which evoked both the glory of the short-lived relationship and the big hurt I felt. I wondered what girl had stolen his heart.

I had a successful career, a happy marriage, and wonderful children and grandchildren. He receded from my memory, although I remembered his birthday. I grieved for a long time after my mother died. Interestingly, my mother's funeral took place on his birthday.

Now I'm retired, and my children are about the age my mother was when I first brought him home.

For years I thought I might run into him somewhere, especially when I went to the theater, the opera, or an independent film; I figured that's where he would be. Or perhaps at a political rally. I always thought it would be when I wasn't wearing any makeup, so I made sure to look my best when I went to those places. But it never happened. It's probably just as well, because what do you say to a person who simply disappeared from your life without any explanation? Clearly, the attraction had not been mutual.

But still, you can't stop remembering. Part of the mystery was trying to figure out what I had done wrong. Why did I drive him away? What had I said or done—or not done?

Nothing, I finally realized.

The world was very different then. Back then, the rules were the rules. People flouted them at their own peril. Love was between a man and a woman. Boys were boys and girls were girls.

It's different now. Times have changed. Everything is out in the open. It's a good thing. No one has to pretend.

No one has to get hurt.

14

The Lifespan of Dolls

Marjorie and Her "Creepy" Dolls

My granddaughter, Jessica, is in the third grade. She's smart, funny, and best of all, she looks like me. Maybe not now, but when I was eight. She has a long brown ponytail, dark brown eyes, and a smile that melts my heart. Her latest passion is Squishmallows, those soft, cuddly, colorful, and mushy figures. They're sort of a combination between a stuffed animal and a pillow. And there's barely room on her bed for her growing collection. Her parents can't understand her obsession, and at first, I didn't either.

Nevertheless, I keep buying them for her, and her parents are threatening to send her and all the Squishmallows to live with me. Actually, I wouldn't mind.

When I was Jessica's age, every morning after my mother made my bed, she lined up my dolls on my pink bedspread. There were Ginny dolls, and her baby sister, Ginnette, Tiny Tears, Raggedy Ann, Barbie, a bride doll, and assorted stuffed animals and "little people." I named them all and they all became characters in the plays my brother and I staged. They were assigned ages and religions and went to public school, Catholic school, and Hebrew school. Sometimes they went to the hospital or a party. And we used my brother's blocks to build edifices in which they attended these activities.

When I got my period at eleven and my mother told me it meant I was a woman, I was afraid I would have to stop playing with my dolls. But she said I could play with them as long as I wanted to. Which I did.

Before my daughter, Deborah—my fourth child and only daughter—was born, I used to fantasize about how I would have a little girl who would love dolls. Unfortunately, once she was old enough, she showed me that she wasn't one for playing with dolls. Having three older brothers, she loved LEGO, horseplay, and playing ball games with them.

Still, I continued to collect dolls—even as an adult—in the hope that she would change her mind at some point. But she didn't. In high school she followed in the footsteps of her brothers; she was an athlete, playing tennis and softball. She also attended ballet lessons for three weeks when she was six and then refused to go. My dreams of applauding at dance recitals while Deborah whirled by in a pink tutu with pink satin shoes were quickly dashed.

It was at that point that I bought myself a ballerina doll. I decided that because I loved dolls so much, I could keep collecting them even if my daughter didn't share my passion. I continued to collect them and soon learned that there were doll magazines to read and even doll shows to attend. A teacher colleague of mine, Ethel, introduced me to them. She was single and in her sixties, and her hobby was collecting dolls. She taught me about QVC, where I could see and order dolls on the TV at any hour of the day or night. She even took me to a doll show where I purchased a Scarlett O'Hara doll. She was about sixteen inches tall and wore an emerald-green gown with a ruffled petticoat and a matching hat and shoes. Later, from QVC, I bought a Dorothy doll from *The Wizard of Oz* in a blue-and-white checked dress holding her dog, Toto. There were many others I accumulated over the years, including Howdy Doody, a Victorian lady, an Inuit, and a Native American in traditional dress, which we bought in Arizona.

When we moved to our gated community, I continued collecting and convinced myself that the dolls weren't just for me; someday I would have a granddaughter who would appreciate them as much as I did.

I designated one of the bedrooms in our new condominium as a room for our grandchildren. We painted it a bright turquoise with a white trundle bed and white furniture. On the bed, I lined up the dolls that our future granddaughter could play with. And we had shelves built to showcase the collector's items. I was so proud of the room we had put together.

But Jessica isn't interested in dolls—only Squishmallows. In fact, I asked her whether she wanted an American Girl doll for her birthday. I told her we could go to the store in Manhattan together with her mother, pick out the doll, have her ears pierced, and then go to lunch in the American Girl café there. But she said, "No thank you, Grammy. I just want more Squishmallows."

The last time she slept at our home in the turquoise room, she woke me up crying in the middle of the night. She stood by my bed, sobbing.

"Grammy, your dolls are creepy," she cried, barely able to catch her breath. "I can't sleep. Can you get rid of them?"

Get rid of them? I thought to myself. How awful. This was like the "Living Doll" episode of *The Twilight Zone* with Talky Tina featuring Telly Savalas, who played a tough guy scared of a doll. I remember how terrified I had been when I first saw that show as a youngster.

At her insistence, and because her crying broke my heart, I quickly stashed Howdy Doody, my beautiful Madame Alexander baby doll, and an old-fashioned lady with a hat and a long dress in the closet in another room.

I stayed up for hours analyzing this turn of events. Had the dolls absorbed some of my childhood trauma? Would it rub off on my granddaughter? How could she not love my dolls as I did? What would she say to me in the morning?

The next morning she asked for chocolate chip pancakes and chocolate milk. When I said, "Of course," she giggled.

"Can we go to the pool later, Grammy?" she asked. "And can I order grilled cheese and french fries at the snack bar?"

"Yes. Sounds like a plan."

Later, as we sat outside at the snack bar eating lunch, I couldn't quite fathom how this feminine little girl who wore dresses to school and bows in her hair simply didn't like dolls. She was eclectic in her tastes; she loved making jewelry and drawing and lacrosse and basketball and softball and baking, but she had rejected my loves.

Most of my dolls are now relegated to the closet, the orphans of changing tastes and norms. It's much better that my granddaughter is growing up in a world where she can choose what she likes and she is free to express her opinion. But I'm going to let her know where they are in the hope that her own children may one day want to play with them.

15
Nobody's Child

Marjorie went shopping in her closet for a black dress as all the children gathered in their childhood home to prepare for the funeral of Alice, Marjorie's mother and their grandmother. This was the house where newborn babies had been brought home from the hospital, where the four children took their first steps, where birthday and anniversary parties were held, where achievements were applauded, and disappointments shared. It was the house where Alice had visited several times a week when Marjorie needed help and support while she was overwhelmed with the demands of babies and children. Now it would be a house of shiva once again.

Marjorie and her brother had learned the ropes only two years earlier when their father Albert died after a long illness. Alice and Albert, the dynamic duo—a good-looking and smart team—had been severed. But Albert had outlived everyone's expectations, surviving for ten years after his initial diagnosis. Marjorie had been confident that her mother would carry on for many years, just as her maternal grandmother, Sadie, had after her grandfather died.

She outlived him by twenty years and died at ninety-two. Marjorie had fully expected her mother to live longer than her grandmother.

Marjorie was a sensitive and anxious person, but she had a steely quality when it came to crises. She would plow through them mechanically and only break down with emotion once they were over. So she supervised as the children covered the mirrors, borrowed a fifty-cup coffee maker from a friend, and went shopping for disposable paper goods.

During the shiva, there was a perpetual stream of guests—from Marjorie and Eric's work to relatives, friends, neighbors, and even visitors for her brother, Barry, and sister-in-law, Trudy, from New Jersey who were sitting shiva with them. The constant crush of visitors was only matched by the mountainous tins of cooked food, cold dishes, cake, cookies, and rugelach.

And then the shiva was over. The endless visitors—along with all the children and Barry and Trudy—left, and it was time to resume life again.

Marjorie tried to put on a happy face for her fourth-grade students and her colleagues. Another fourth-grade teacher, who had lost her father the year before, gave her a card with "The Mourner's Bill of Rights" on it. One thing it said was that grief has no timetable. Did that mean she would be in this funk forever? She noted that this was different than the Jewish mourning perspective, which had a pace and rhythm spread out over eleven months. When it ended, you were no longer a mourner.

How could she admit to anyone that she was fifty-eight years old and was now bereft without her mother? Alice had been her right arm, her best friend, her most loyal confidante. Who could possibly know that she had repeated every word of what happened every day in her life to her mother? Every conversation in the faculty room, every parent interaction, every directive from the principal, every discipline problem, every achievement of not only her four children but her students, too. And certainly every argument she had with Eric or anyone else.

Marjorie was grateful that her three sons had not only shown up for the funeral and shiva—some even flying in from out of state—but also spoke so beautifully about their beloved grandmother and even took turns leading the shiva minyans in their living room. Eric was quite supportive too—and he even dissolved into tears at the funeral. She knew he truly loved her mother, and she loved him. She couldn't remember him crying at his own father's funeral.

Deborah did all the daughterly things expected of her—bringing her mother plates of food, making coffee, setting up and cleaning up, and chatting with the visitors.

Yes, Marjorie was blessed, but now she was depressed. She called her best friend, Linda, who lived a few communities away in Syosset and was also a teacher. They had grown up together, first meeting in kindergarten and going all the way through college and graduate school together.

"Your mother was so wonderful," Linda said. "So wise and loving. I always secretly wished that she was my mother. Of course, I loved my mother; isn't it written somewhere that you have to? But yours was so put together, so smart, so American. She didn't have all that Holocaust refugee baggage my mother carried.

"I think today they'd call my mother clinically depressed," Linda continued as if Marjorie had never met her mother. "And then, of course, the nightmares, the anxiety I had to talk her through. It was almost as if I was her mother."

"I'm sorry, Linda," Marjorie said, now finding herself in the strange position of apologizing to Linda for her own perfect mother. This had the effect of making her feel worse.

"We should get together for dinner," Linda said. "Or are you not up to it yet?"

Linda had given her an out; she simply couldn't see how she was going to sit in a restaurant with her and continue this line of conversation.

"Thanks, Linda. I think it's too soon."

Marjorie hung up the phone and dissolved into tears. Why had she thought Linda would have the right words for her? She meant well; she thought she was being kind. But Marjorie had wanted to talk about her mother, not Linda's.

Who could she talk to? She tried Barry, and he listened attentively to Marjorie's woeful words. And she felt momentarily comforted that at least her brother was a good listener. He was a person who kept all the friends he ever had and was constantly helping them solve their problems.

"I feel so old," Marjorie said. "I never felt old when Mom was alive. Now I'm no one's daughter. I feel like I'm going to die."

"We're all going to die," Barry said. "But I think you've got a long way to go. In any case, I think coming face-to-face with your own mortality isn't necessarily a bad thing."

But he was grieving too, and soon the conversation devolved into what else they might have done, what they had done wrong. Was it their fault their mother had died? Should they have forced her into a clinical trial? Taken her out of state to another hospital? Why hadn't either of them noticed sooner that something was seriously wrong?

Finally, Barry said, "Marjorie, I have to get back to work. Let's talk again soon."

There was no point in calling any of her children. Marjorie had tried that route already. She was shocked and actually quite hurt that none of the four—not even Deborah—wanted to hear about her grief. She realized that even though she had spent their entire lives listening to and helping solve their problems, they just couldn't cope with their mother being so sad and vulnerable. Each of them had responded to her in the same way: "You should go for therapy, Mom."

"Do you think I need to go for therapy?" Marjorie asked Eric that night.

"No, of course not," he said.

Marjorie knew that despite the torrent of tears at Alice's funeral, Eric did not talk about feelings, nor did he want to talk about hers.

"So many of my friends go," Marjorie continued, "but it's something I've never considered. Maybe because my mother had such a therapeutic personality, I didn't think I needed it. I always felt calmed and comforted when I shared my problems with her."

A couple of days later, Marjorie stopped into ShopRite on the way home from school. She needed some lettuce and other fixings for Eric's salad. As she was trying to decide whether to buy a bag of salad mix to make it easy on her or a head of lettuce, she spotted Irene, a woman about her age she knew from Hadassah. Irene gave Marjorie a friendly hello and introduced her to the older woman who was with her.

"This is my mother, Rose," Irene said.

"Nice to meet you, Marjorie," said Rose. "What do you recommend—the bag of salad or the head of lettuce?"

Other than a walker, Marjorie thought the woman who stood next to Irene looked amazing. And she was a quick study! Her hair was dyed a medium brown and it looked like it had been professionally done. She had on a bit of eye makeup, powder, blush, and lipstick and was dressed in a nice blouse and pants. Marjorie noted that she looked fancier than her daughter, who wore a T-shirt and jeans with long, unstyled hair and no makeup.

"Oh, I think the head," Marjorie said. "I was just checking out both and I don't like the dates on the bags. I decided on the head."

"They're a little depleted here by the afternoon," Rose said. "But I went with Irene this morning to visit my great-grandson and we had lunch there. Irene, next time we should come earlier."

"I was sorry to hear about your mother," Irene said, changing the subject.

"Thank you."

"Oh, you lost your mother. That's the worst," Rose said as she leaned forward and touched Marjorie's hand. "I remember when I lost mine. She was only sixty. How old was your mother?"

"She was eighty-five."

"There's never enough time with your mother. I'm turning ninety-three next month and I've been without my mother for sixty years. Thankfully, I have a wonderful daughter."

Marjorie eked out a "God bless you," but then was stricken speechless. *Sure, maybe that's true. But look at you and your daughter. She has a protective shell around her because her mother is still alive. When your mother is alive, you think you are younger than you are because you are still someone's child. Both my parents are dead; I am nobody's child.*

"Well, we better get going, Ma," Irene said to Rose. "Again, Marjorie, I'm so sorry for your loss."

"Yes," said Rose. "Just remember that because your mother isn't with you physically anymore, she's still with you in many ways. And always remember to count your blessings."

So full of emotion, Marjorie almost stumbled as she walked to her car in the parking lot with her one bag of produce. Once inside she sobbed, allowing her tears to wash over her. She cried for the mother she could no longer confide in on a daily basis. She cried that her children wanted her to seek professional help instead of listening to her themselves.

She tried to count her blessings. A loyal and loving husband. A growing family. Good health, faith, friends, community. Her mother's wisdom, which was always with her. She remembered her brother's words: *Coming face-to-face with your own mortality isn't necessarily a bad thing.*

It makes you think about the bigger picture and your own legacy, she thought. *It inspires you not only to give, but also to live.* All true, she thought, but still it wouldn't be easy. She thought of the amputees featured on the evening news who figured out how to do great things after losing a limb. She would have to find a way to go on without the symbolic right arm she had come to rely upon her entire life.

But not now—she was only ten days out from the funeral. She was entitled to her grief. Her cell phone rang and she saw it was Eric.

"Hi, hon, what's up?" she asked.

"Looks like another orthopedic emergency," he said. "I'll be tied up most of the night."

"What are you talking about, midnight?"

"Hopefully by then."

Marjorie started sobbing again.

"Oh, don't cry. What's wrong?"

"I feel so alone."

"You know I love you," he said. "Pick up something delicious for dinner and have a glass of wine."

"Sure," she said, and hung up the phone.

She returned home to a dark, empty house. When her mother was alive, she would call her as soon as she took her coat off. She noticed that their colonial had become too big for just her and Eric. Perhaps they should look into a gated community, where the landscaping and snow removal would be taken care of by the homeowner's association, and the neighbors were close by.

She headed for the kitchen and turned on the light. *There must be something in the freezer from the shiva,* she thought.

As she surveyed the contents of the freezer, the phone rang.

"Hi, Marjorie, it's Jonah Rothberg. I'm so sorry I didn't get to make it to you for the shiva. You know I was in Israel for my uncle's funeral."

"Please, Jonah, don't mention it. Of course you went to Israel for your family. Anyway, Andrea was here—twice. She was so helpful; she picked up paper goods for me and loaned me your fifty-cup coffee urn."

"Well, let me bring dinner for you and Eric tonight. Andrea is playing mah jongg, and I'll pick up the coffee pot."

"Of course, you can get the coffee pot, or I can drop it off tomorrow if you need it. As far as dinner goes, Eric isn't home; he has an emergency surgery. He'll probably be at the hospital at least until midnight."

"Well, in that case, let me bring you dinner and keep you company for a bit. I know how difficult it is to be alone right after a loss. I insist."

"Are you sure?"

"A hundred percent. What would you like?"

"Oh, I'm not that hungry these days. What would you like?

"I'm thinking either of kosher Chinese food or pizza. If we do pizza, I'll bring a frozen yogurt pie from TCBY."

"Sounds amazing," said Marjorie. She loved any form of ice cream or frozen yogurt—it was her number one comfort food.

Marjorie began to clean off the kitchen counters. During the shiva, her friends and relatives had kept the kitchen sparkling; left to her own devices, she didn't care. But now she did; Jonah Rothberg was paying her a visit.

If the truth be told, there had always been an attraction between Jonah and Marjorie. Her astute friend Robin had pulled her aside after a synagogue board meeting a couple of years ago and told her that she had noticed the chemistry between the two of them.

"I can tell the way you and Jonah look at each other," she said. "You ought to try to control it—you don't want people talking."

Marjorie was horrified. "What are you, a witch or something?"

"I am, I notice everything. Probably others don't, but as your friend, I'm telling you to try to be less obvious."

"But there's absolutely nothing going on," Marjorie insisted.

"What's going on is a symbolic affair."

Marjorie thought about Robin's accusation long and hard. And Robin was a good friend. She had to take her warning at face value.

She had to admit she was intrigued with Jonah. He was the exact opposite of Eric. Eric was a man of few words. He didn't gossip or, for that matter, have that much to say. And he didn't have such great patience for Marjorie's stories. He called them *lashon hara*.

"Eric loves you. He's such a good man, he has no guile. He will never cheat on you," her mother used to tell her when she got angry at him.

And Marjorie knew her husband was all those things. But she enjoyed the *yenta*-ing after the board meetings and also the conversation about substantive issues. She liked to perseverate. Eric, as a physician, was a bottom-line kind of guy. She especially enjoyed "the meeting after the meeting" when she and Jonah and three or four others would go to the diner and sit and talk, sometimes until two in the morning. And Eric trusted her so much, he would invariably be tight asleep when she returned home.

About forty-five minutes later, Jonah appeared at her door with a bottle of Marjorie's favorite Chardonnay, a pizza that was half plain and half mushroom, a Greek salad, and a cookies-and-cream yogurt pie.

A criminal attorney, he was shorter than Eric and balding, but he had an infectious smile and gregarious personality.

"What did you do? This is too much for two people." Marjorie smiled as she surveyed the huge amount of food he had brought for them.

"Just want to cheer you up a bit. I'm sure you can use it. And I'm sure Eric will enjoy the leftovers."

They sat at the kitchen table and ate and sipped the wine, and Marjorie became more relaxed.

Jonah shared his own losses and difficulties. His father had died two years ago, and his uncle had been the last sibling on his father's side. His mother had dementia.

She told him that she felt so alone now that her mother was gone.

"Well, you know Andrea and I are always here for you," he said, squeezing her hand.

"I know and I appreciate it," she said as she felt a spark of electricity.

Their conversation switched to synagogue politics.

Once the chairperson of the catering committee, Jonah lamented, "No one wants to have weddings in the shul anymore."

"I know," said Marjorie. "They want destination weddings or vineyards or warehouses in Brooklyn."

They both laughed as Marjorie got up to get a cake knife to cut the pie.

"Let me do it," said Jonah.

She handed him the knife and he cut a large piece and put it on a plate.

"Allow me to offer you the first taste," he said as he dug a fork into the pie and moved his chair as close as was physically possible to Marjorie's and fed her a piece.

"Yum," she said, "so sweet and delicious."

"Just like you," he said. "Now you feed it to me."

Marjorie was feeling warm and giddy from the wine and she complied.

He touched her knee as the pie melted in his mouth.

"Now it's my turn," Jonah said with a big grin as he fed her another mouthful.

He put his hand over hers and said, "I know how close you were to your mom. I'm here for you."

"This has been a real treat, Jonah. Thanks so much for coming over."

"Is that my cue to exit?"

"I wish you didn't have to go, but it's getting late."

They both got up and walked to the door.

The two stood there silently and Jonah took both of Marjorie's hands and looked into her eyes.

"You've always been very special to me," he said.

Then he cupped her head in his hands and kissed her on the cheek.

"You are a woman who is beautiful inside and out."

And then he kissed her on the lips, and she didn't resist.

He kissed her on the lips again and this time his tongue explored her mouth.

She grabbed him tighter. She did not want this to end.

It was Jonah who decided to call it quits.

"I better go," he said. "It's getting late."

Marjorie was disappointed and relieved at the same time.

He kissed her hand, opened the door, and left.

Suddenly, Marjorie remembered the coffee pot that he had forgotten to take. *Would he come back for it another day?*

She walked into the kitchen and surveyed the evidence. She had better get rid of this before Eric came home. She tore up the pizza box and threw it and the leftover pizza and salad into a bag. Luckily the garbage would be taken tomorrow morning. She brought the can to the curb.

She didn't have the heart to throw away the TCBY pie. She reasoned that if she cut it into pieces and stashed it in the refrigerator in the garage, Eric would never know the difference.

But she did.

Marjorie could still feel the excitement of being kissed by Jonah. She felt daring and attractive and alive. And she knew that this would be the one thing she could never have told her mother.

16

Security in the Sunshine State

When Grandma Sadie died in 1978, Marjorie spoke at her funeral. She talked about how her grandmother had been born into a world without electricity and died after men walked on the moon. At the time, Marjorie believed that it was the period of greatest technological progress ever. But now, she was not so sure. She looked at her cell phone waiting for Deborah to return her text. No one wanted to talk on the phone anymore. She wistfully recalled her own frequent and lengthy conversations with her mother. But now she would ring and ring and none of her four children would even pick up the phone. They only wanted to text.

Gone were the days when she would have hour-long conversations with Deborah. Her daughter was much too busy now with her own life, her child, and her career. Marjorie loved the sweet pictures her three daughters-in-law were kind enough to text her of her adorable grandkids doing cute things. Occasionally they would FaceTime and the children would say a few words and throw kisses, but they weren't exactly loquacious on FaceTime.

Marjorie was comforted knowing that she was not alone in this. Her friends reassured her that texting—not speaking on the phone—was the norm among their children too. In fact, she had read an article recently that the preferred method of communication among young people was texting. Most of them didn't even have a landline anymore. And just as email had replaced the fine art of letter writing, so too had texting replaced the phone.

Thankfully, Marjorie's kids were pretty good about visiting her and Eric and inviting them to their own homes in the city or on Long Island or Westchester. The thought of not seeing her grandchildren on a regular basis upset Marjorie. It was better than a glass of Chardonnay or a hot fudge sundae. The kids were all growing so fast; she didn't want to miss a single milestone.

That was just one of many reasons Marjorie fought the idea of spending winters in Florida, especially when Eric insisted that, after his open-heart surgery, he simply could not tolerate another season of northeast blizzards. They had had this conversation on numerous occasions, and this time they were sitting in the Moonbeam Diner eating pancakes.

"But in New York," Marjorie insisted, "I can at least see the grandchildren in the flesh. If we spend the winters in Florida, the most we can hope for would be one visit from each of our kids and their families."

"It's no less than we're seeing them now. And we're all living in the metropolitan area. Plus in Florida it's more than a three-hour afternoon visit. They'd be living with us for at least a week."

There was no comeback to his reasoning. But the truth was that Marjorie never really "got" Florida. She never understood why senior citizens would leave the northeast in droves to either become snowbirds (there for the winter) or relocate there, when their children were elsewhere. Her paternal grandmother, Essie, became a Florida resident in the 1960s. Marjorie could picture Essie's tiny efficiency apartment in what is now South Beach. The thought of it depressed her. Especially when she compared her to Grandma Sadie, who came to live with Marjorie and her family when her husband, Mayer, died. Sadie was an integral part of their family, and she found lots of activities to engage her at the local JCC Golden Age Club.

On the other hand, Marjorie's in-laws had permanently settled in the Sunshine State around the turn of the twenty-first century. Over the coming years, so did numerous relatives, friends, and neighbors, many going so far as becoming Florida residents and claiming that they didn't mind the scorching August temperatures.

Lately, more of their friends and neighbors had retired and moved to Florida. They, too, continued to sing its praises to her and Eric, especially the weather and the tax benefits. She could see that Eric lapped up all this Florida PR and that it bolstered his resolve to pressure her to move south.

Even if she agreed to go for the winter, Marjorie vowed she would never become a Florida resident. She suspected that her prejudice against the Sunshine State was probably influenced by her parents' view that it was a cultural wasteland for old people. And, of course, who could forget Jerry Seinfeld's hilarious depiction of Del Boca Vista, the fictional condominium community where his parents resided?

"Florida is not the same as when your grandmother lived there—and you know it," Eric said. "We have friends living in gorgeous communities. And they're incredibly active; they're so busy they don't even seem to miss their kids. There are lectures and concerts and Broadway-quality plays. And as far as the *Seinfeld* episode, you don't see a lot of early-bird dinners anymore, but you do see a lot of old people in the restaurants. And that's a good thing—that people are out and about in their nineties and beyond. Look at my mother's friend Irene Silver; she's going to be 103. Maybe people are just living longer there."

"I will never become a Florida resident," Marjorie vowed.

"Okay, you don't have to. But I really can't stand the cold winters."

"The winters have been milder."

"But you can't guarantee that."

Marjorie had enough of her mother in her that she knew she would have to give in to her husband. Alice had been a peacemaker, catering to her husband, suppressing her own desires.

And during their month-long visits to Florida in previous years, Marjorie had actually enjoyed herself, especially connecting with friends and family. Besides, Eric was in love with the local shul. Not only did it have magnificent Shabbat services with amazing rabbis, cantors, and choir, there were so many activities, classes, and lectures that he could spend a good part of every day there. And while Marjorie loved her home synagogue, she also was impressed with the vast array of offerings in the Florida shul.

Driving her car on Jericho Turnpike, she mulled over the pros and cons. She noted to herself that in Florida everything would be fresh and new with few memories attached. *Is that why old people want to be there?* she wondered. On Long Island, everything evoked memories.

She drove past Selmer's Pet Land—the site of the very first nursery-school field trip for the twins. The sign read IN BUSINESS SINCE 1939—NOW PERMANENTLY CLOSED. She passed one of the few Friendly's that was still open; many of them had been shuttered. She used to take the kids for lunch there. They would get the kids grilled cheese, french fries, and a drink for about a dollar. She thought of the rapid passage of time, and she felt old.

Maybe that's why people in Florida didn't feel so old. They were surrounded by their peers, and seventy looked young next to ninety or one hundred.

And there were no landmarks by which to measure your aging. For instance, the supermarkets were different. Even Trader Joe's had a different vibe in Florida. *Here on Long Island, I feel like the old grandmother shopping in Denny's for baby gifts. I used to be the young mother when it first opened.* In Florida, everyone was the youthful grandma—either by healthy eating, exercise, cosmetic surgery, or attitude.

Of course, it was just a matter of time until Marjorie gave in to Eric, and they agreed to rent an apartment in a midrise building in a luxury gated community for four months—just to see whether they liked the Florida lifestyle.

The first lesson she learned was that golf was somewhat of a religion there. The country club community was set on an eighteen-hole golf course with a shop that sold golf clothes, shoes, and golf equipment for men and women, making it somewhat irreverent not to at least attempt to play the game. Residents drove around the community in their golf carts. Eric had played before, but now Marjorie, never having been much of an athlete, joined a beginner's clinic.

The apartment they rented was pristine; it was furnished in typical Florida style—everything in white and clean and fresh. It had two bedrooms, a den, and two bathrooms, just enough space to host family visits. It seemed that most of the neighbors in the building kept to themselves. The day they moved in, a man and woman, who both looked fit and in their sixties, rang their bell and introduced themselves. Sol and Vivian Bergman said that they lived directly across the hall and hailed from New Jersey. He was a retired stockbroker, and she had been an interior decorator. Right away they insisted on making a date with Marjorie and Eric to dine in one of the country club's two restaurants. After they left, Eric noted that they were a very smiley and friendly couple.

"I'm not sure," Marjorie said.

"Now what?" Eric asked in exasperation. "You're just determined not to like it here."

"That's not true. You know I'm a witch. There was just something in his eyes I didn't like."

"Oh, just stop it, please."

A few evenings later, Sol insisted on driving the four of them to the Coach Restaurant, and Marjorie had to admit that she was impressed by the décor of the venue and the menu. It looked like a very upscale sports bar with large-screen TVs all over the dining room. There was a salad bar, a pizza station, and another with Carvel. *The grandkids are going to love this,* she thought to herself. She was pleased that there were many fish and vegetarian dishes on the menu, since they didn't eat meat.

Vivian was a bit quiet, and Sol did most of the talking. He raved about the community and said he would show them the ropes. He was glad they were taking golf lessons, but that was only the beginning.

"There's a men's poker game, Eric, and do you guys play canasta?"

"No, we don't," Marjorie replied. "We're really not card players."

"Well, we have couples' canasta here. It's on Wednesday nights. We'll teach you both. Then we can have dinner together in the club every week before the game. And if you want to learn pickleball, that's fun also."

"Eric had open-heart surgery. I don't think that's such a good idea for him."

"I understand, but there's plenty more to do. There's a special interest club every week during the season, which hosts interesting speakers. Maybe you want to do a talk about orthopedics, Eric."

"We'll see. We need to get settled; we just got here," Eric said.

Vivian shared with Marjorie the pros and cons of getting her hair and nails done at the club or at a local salon.

Eric was very perky after the dinner. But Marjorie wasn't thrilled about being co-opted by what she perceived as a controlling guy who didn't make eye contact. She was relieved when her son Josh, his wife, and two kids came to visit during the winter vacation. It would give them a break from Sol. The grandchildren were thrilled with the facilities, especially the huge swimming pool and snack bar, where they ran to get treats.

On the Sabbath after the kids left, Marjorie and Eric went to the synagogue and were warmly greeted by the rabbi, who asked them how they were settling in.

"We notice that almost everyone is Jewish."

"Yes," said the rabbi. "There are a lot of Jews here. That's why the police are particularly concerned, especially after

October 7 and the increase in antisemitic incidents and rhetoric. As you know, we've ramped up security here."

They took their seats in the sanctuary. In his sermon, the rabbi spoke about the increased antisemitism and the importance of vigilance. Halfway through his sermon, one of the ushers raced down the side aisle, ascended the steps of the bima, and hurriedly walked up to the rabbi and whispered in his ear.

Seconds later, the rabbi turned and told the congregation, "Please be calm and exit the building quickly using all the exits here in front and on the side. I've just been informed that the police are here and they've asked us to evacuate the building because of a bomb threat."

"I told you we shouldn't have come to Florida," Marjorie said as she pushed Eric to move faster out of the building.

"This has nothing to do with Florida," Eric replied, raising his voice. "Unfortunately, it's everywhere."

Twenty minutes later, the police announced that the building had been searched and they were now free to return to the service.

Once inside, the rabbi stepped up to the podium and announced, "We want to assure you that everyone is safe, and all appropriate measures were taken to address the situation. We have now received the all-clear from our police. They have informed me that our synagogue, along with approximately fifty others in the state of Florida, received a bomb threat via email. Our security team, in collaboration with our local law enforcement, responded promptly and efficiently to ensure the safety of everyone here."

Once they returned to the apartment, the phone rang throughout the afternoon. Each of their four children called to check on them. But Marjorie became more and more distraught.

"We have to get out of here," she insisted. "Can you imagine how bad this is? All of our kids actually picked up the phone and called. They didn't just text. It's all over the news. They're worried about us. Let's go home."

"We're not going home," Eric said. "You're starting to like it. It's a great life here and these dangers are everywhere; there's no escaping it. And think about it, you got a chance to speak with each of the kids. That's one way to get them to call."

17

Possibility and Privilege

Marjorie's Story

My thirty-seven-year-old daughter Deborah is my fourth child and my only daughter. She is brilliant and beautiful. She has hazel eyes and auburn hair, which is straight and thick and long. She is naturally lean, never having to struggle with her weight the way I have for as long as I can remember. From the day she was born, her entire path has been pregnant with possibility and potential and promise. She is the embodiment and the fulfillment of all my hopes and dreams and aspirations. She is blessed to have been born in a time when her older brothers paved the path for her in a society that welcomed the contributions of women. Doors were open and opportunities arrived at her feet like wrapped birthday presents.

She is a lawyer with a degree from an Ivy League law school. She works for a white-shoe law firm. She has a husband and two children. She has hot and cold running help.

She lives in a three-bedroom apartment with a doorman on the Upper East Side. The world has always been her oyster.

I want to tell her that only a generation ago, she would have had to scrape and struggle to accomplish her dreams. *I know, I was there, and I saw that society did not accommodate professional women back then.* She would have had to scrounge to find daycare for her children. She would have been suspect in a man's profession. She would not have been available to take her children to birthday parties and playdates. And she would have been perpetually missing or late to daytime school events and meetings because she was at work. That was the lot for the very few female doctors and lawyers and other professional women back in my day.

And I want her to know that in her grandmother's time, the path she chose would have been an even more precarious and lonely one. And as for her great-grandmother, one of twelve, born on Hester Street on the Lower East Side, it would have been unthinkable.

But Deborah has no idea how privileged and entitled she is, and she needs to know. From the time she was a child, she has listened to my stories and lived my dreams.

But now I'm going to tell her what really happened when I wanted to—but didn't—go to law school.

"I don't understand why you didn't just go," she always says whenever we have this conversation. "No one tied you up or locked you in a closet and prevented you from going."

"Easy for you to say, you weren't there," I replied. "You don't understand what it was like."

"Why did you become a teacher if you wanted to be a lawyer? It doesn't make sense to me."

"I was thinking of going," I said. "I majored in political science and I was fascinated with government. I was one of only four girls in my political science classes. All of my friends were majoring in elementary education. At the end of my junior year, I made an appointment to see the law advisor. I told him I was thinking of going to law school.

"His name was Dr. Pemberton. He had dark brown hair and black horn-rimmed glasses. He was clean-shaven. When I entered his office, he was sitting behind his desk, wearing a plaid sports jacket and puffing on his pipe. He invited me to sit down and he looked me up and down and thought for a minute. I was wearing a mini dress, which was the style back then, and suddenly became conscious that he was looking at my legs. I uncrossed my legs and tried to pull the dress down.

"'You'd make a very attractive lawyer,' he said, with a leering smile. 'A couple of women apply each year, and you do have fabulous grades. You know you'd have to take the LSATs, but I don't think that would be a problem for you. But let me be honest, the women who apply, they're not like you; they don't look like you. They're resigned to acting like men in a man's world. It's almost impossible to take care of a husband and family and devote yourself to a career in law. Do you really want to become a lawyer or do you want to go to law school to find a husband?'

"I was speechless. How could I possibly answer this question? I thought I wanted to be a lawyer. But I also wanted to eventually get married and have children.

"The only female lawyer I knew was my mother's first cousin Edith. She was about five years younger than my mother and she boasted that she was a member of Mensa. She made it a point to tell everyone about it so they would appreciate how smart she was. She lived alone in a cluttered apartment in Greenwich Village. She had a high, squeaky voice and she weighed about three hundred pounds. My mother said she had a voice that sounded like Baby Snooks. Baby Snooks was before my time, but she was a child character played by Fanny Brice on the radio.

"Edith was very nice to me when my mother told her I was thinking of going to law school. She invited me to a lawyers' dinner in Manhattan. It was Edith and me in a sea of men with a handful of women scattered here and there. Everyone at our table, except for us, was a man. I was so embarrassed when Edith got drunk and fell off her chair. At the table was a mature judge, who had also consumed a few drinks too many. He kept telling me how pretty I was, and that I'd probably get married and drop out of law school if I went.

"'If you just want to marry a lawyer, there are other ways to meet one,' said Dr. Pemberton. 'You could be a legal secretary or a court reporter. But honestly, the best career for a woman is a teacher. You could be a social studies teacher, so you'd be using your major. You'd have the summers off.'

"I was filled with despair. Dr. Pemberton was beginning to sound like my mother. Except that he suggested that I first teach in Europe for a couple of years. 'I can picture you driving around in a little red sports car.' He clearly didn't get me."

"So you listened to that jerk?" Deborah asked. "He was a male chauvinist pig. Wasn't it illegal to talk like that?"

"No, not back then. That's how people talked. Even my own mother, who was a college grad and a World War II veteran, believed that. I think she was afraid I would end up like Edith. Why, I have no idea. I had nothing in common with Edith. But my mother—for some reason, and I wished I had asked her this when she was alive—was afraid that I wouldn't get married if I became a lawyer. She said, 'Don't outclass yourself.' The irony is that your father would have been fine with me being a lawyer; he's always empowered me in everything I've wanted to do."

"Then why didn't you go after you were married?"

"Good question. By the time I was ready to go back to school I was in my forties, and people told me that I'd never get a decent job as a lawyer at that age. I believed this to be true. I have a friend who went at that age, and all she could get was a recruiting job—finding positions for younger lawyers."

"Seems like you were easily dissuaded. I don't think you were passionate enough."

"Probably so, or just afraid."

"Afraid of what?"

"I don't know, maybe failing."

"Well, you could have just done it for yourself. You could have just tried it. And what was the story when they asked you to run for office? Why didn't you do that either?"

"That wasn't my fault. I wanted to do it. You know Scott Rosner, he's our representative in Congress now? Well, back in the day he was a political operative, and he asked me to have lunch with him and another political activist at the Moonbeam Diner.

"As I ate my Greek salad, Scott asked me if I had ever considered running for office. I said that was my secret dream. Then Lenny Simon, the other guy, told me that the party was looking to run a woman with high visibility in the Jewish community and they thought of me. He wanted to know if I would be willing to do what it takes to run for office. I quickly answered that I would.

"Then Scott, who was a member of our shul, asked me if I would be willing to campaign on Shabbat. He said: 'You know, you'd have to go to the supermarkets and the malls and pump the flesh on the weekends. That's very important. You're personable; the voters will like you.'

"I quickly answered that we had a family Shabbat dinner each Friday night and took the children to synagogue on Saturday.

"Lenny frowned and said, 'I'll have to run this by Carmine Pizzimenti. He's the county Democratic chairman. He insists that all of our candidates are out campaigning seven days a week. I'll check with him, but please think this over; we think you'd be a winning candidate.'

"I went home and discussed this with Dad. 'That's absurd,' he said. 'They're asking you to run because you have high visibility in the Jewish community, in the shul, in the day school, in UJA, in Hadassah. You're a role model. And they want you to leave your family and campaign on Shabbos. Doesn't make sense; I bet Carmine will understand.'

"I waited and waited for a call from Scott or from Lenny. I dreamed of running, winning, and later becoming a member of Congress."

"How old was I when this happened?"

"You were about four."

"Was the job full-time? Was there a salary?"

"It was considered part-time and it was local, and there was what seemed to me a decent salary for what I would be doing.

"A couple of weeks went by and I kept leaving messages for both of them. Finally, Lenny called me and told me that Carmine said that not campaigning on the Sabbath was a deal-breaker. I guess Scott was too embarrassed to call. Dad was outraged, but Grandma was relieved. She insisted that I didn't have a thick enough skin for politics and my children were too young for such an undertaking.

"I was very disappointed, but felt I had no recourse. The party chose another Jewish woman, who was a lawyer in her fifties. She lost.

"A few years later, Joe Lieberman was in the Senate, making it very clear that he did not work on Shabbat, and everyone respected that. What was even more unbelievable was that eventually that seat would be held by an Orthodox yarmulke-wearing man, who clearly did not campaign on Shabbos."

"Well, that's a sad story," Deborah said with a frown. "I'm really sorry. But what I don't understand is why you gave up? Why didn't you try again later? There were so many women in politics only a few years later. Aunt Trudy's cousin Susan was elected to Congress."

"I just didn't have the confidence you have. I didn't understand the possibilities or the speed at which things were changing. I looked at everything as either/or. I went back to teaching and that was it."

"And did Scott ever say anything about what happened?"

"Not at the time, but interestingly, I ran into him recently and he brought it up. I was so surprised that he mentioned it."

"What did he say?"

"He said, 'Marjorie, you know you should have run for the legislature; you would have been great.'"

"But I thought you were disqualified because of your religious observance?" Deborah said.

"So did I; I was shocked that he brought it up, that he was still thinking about it. You know, he's a very big *machar* in Congress and in the party."

"And he remembers it differently than you do," Deborah said.

"Yes, he does. I never thought of it as my choice. I always felt like I had been rejected."

"Well, even if you had been rejected, you could have picked yourself up and tried again, later."

"It never occurred to me," I said.

"Not only that, it seems like you were being discriminated against because of your religious beliefs. That would never happen today. Well, at least you've always been a good mother."

18

Unexpected Blessing

Bobbi Shapiro didn't have an enemy in the world. At just five feet, she had short brown curly hair and was perpetually on a diet. Warm and welcoming, she embraced everyone, both in the school and in the shul, in her neighborhood and beyond. She was the chair of the Social Action Committee at the synagogue and spearheaded clothing and food drives for those less fortunate. She served meals in a soup kitchen once a week and made visits to residents at the local nursing home. She rescued lost pets.

Marjorie often marveled at how Bobbi, her friend and teacher colleague, usually took everything in stride. She didn't seem to have a prejudiced bone in her body. When Bobbi's son Tommy and his husband, Miles, welcomed a baby girl delivered by their surrogate, she was thrilled to become a grandmother for the first time. When her eldest daughter, Rachel, and her Chinese husband, Jun, had twin girls, she proudly showed off photos of the children to everyone she met. People would ooh and aah and say how beautiful they were with their large almond-shaped eyes and straight, silky brown hair. Bobbi would kvell and say, "Aren't their children the perfect combination of the two of them?"

But for some inexplicable reason, Bobbi's third child, her youngest son, Jesse, who was twenty-seven, pushed all of her buttons when he decided to join an ultra-Orthodox sect.

"Why are you so upset?" Marjorie asked her. "You usually take everything your kids do in stride. He's staying in the fold, just a more observant branch."

"But it's so extreme," Bobbi replied. "They don't live in the same world we do. I'm really put off by the way they look. The *peyos* and black hats might have been fashionable in sixteenth-century Poland, but not here. And they are so obviously different that they call attention to themselves when they walk on the street. At least my other two are living in America in the twenty-first century.

"And I'm also very upset by their food restrictions. Even though I have a kosher home, it's not kosher enough for him. It's not just a question of kosher meat. It's the milk, the cheese, even broccoli has to be specially checked for bugs. And even though I have two sets of dishes—one for dairy and one for meat—he won't eat in my house anymore."

"Well, maybe it's just a phase," Marjorie said.

"We can only hope."

Much to Bobbi's chagrin, it was not a phase. Jesse moved to Brooklyn and became enmeshed in an ultra-Orthodox community there. Within three months, the community deemed that he was already past the age of marriage, and *shidduchim* meetings with eligible marriage partners were arranged.

The dates consisted of meeting the prospective spouse in a public place such as the lobby of a hotel. They would sit across from each other at a table and talk to see if they wanted to continue on a second date. No touching was allowed. If they hit it off, they would see each other again. By the end of six dates, if all went well, they would become engaged.

Bobbi called Marjorie in a panic. "They've started with the *shidduchs*. They're going to marry him off and he will be stuck in that community forever."

"So what's so terrible? He'll still be in New York and he and his children will be Jewish."

"He'll be lost to me forever," Bobbi lamented.

"I doubt that," Marjorie said. "There are other people in the shul whose kids have gone that way. They still see them. It's up to you. You always have such a great attitude about everything. Why is this the one thing that's upsetting you so much?"

"I'm not sure, but maybe I don't want every action of mine to be judged for the rest of my life. I consider myself a good Jew. I'm afraid they'll be looking in my pots and cabinets."

Sure enough, Jesse, now called Yishai, found his *bashert* in the form of Chaya Malka Wolfowitz, formerly Cheryl Marlene. She was also a new adherent to this sect. She was twenty-five and overripe for marriage; many in the community already had several children at her age.

"I'm engaged, Mom," Jesse said with a lilt in his voice when his mother picked up the phone.

"Mazel tov," Bobbi automatically replied.

"We're having the *vort* in Brooklyn on Thursday night."

"This Thursday night? Today is Sunday."

"That's the way it's done in the community. You'll meet Chaya Malka and her family. You're going to love her. And be sure to dress modestly."

"Dress modestly? Honestly, Jesse, I'm sixty-five years old."

"Just saying don't wear a pantsuit. Pants on women are not allowed."

"Fine, I'll go shopping in my closet for a dress."

"Make sure it covers your knees."

"Of course, dear, I know what to wear. I wasn't born yesterday," she tried to say in a cheerful voice as she grimaced.

Bobbi hung up the phone and broke the news to her husband, Stanley. He was an accountant who spent a lot of time on the road visiting clients. He was obsessed with traffic.

"Oy; we're going to have to buck the rush-hour traffic to Brooklyn. And what about parking?"

"That's your comment on the situation?" Bobbi was exasperated. "That's what concerns you, the trip to Brooklyn and the parking? Well, you better get used to it, because you're going to be doing it for the rest of your life."

On Friday during their lunch break at the Village School, Marjorie asked Bobbi about how the engagement party had gone.

"It was like being in a foreign country. Chaya Malka is very sweet and her parents seemed normal and as perplexed and confused as we were. They seem just like regular American parents, but their daughter looks and sounds like she was born into it. She wore a long dress, completely covering her clavicle down to her ankles. Her mother must have gotten the memo because she had on a long dress too. My skirt suit was conservative, but it might have been frowned upon because it only covered my knees. And Jesse forgot to tell me that black hose was the accepted style."

"I'm sure you looked lovely," said Marjorie. "You always do. What else can you tell me about besides the clothing?"

"It's just amazing how Chaya Malka has so quickly adopted the speech inflection of her new religious community.

At least Jesse still sounds like himself, but I suppose not for long. The wedding will be in June."

"But that's just three months away. How can you get a venue for this June?"

"It's out of my hands. They have a place. It's one of those ultra-Orthodox catering halls under the El in Brooklyn."

Ten years and seven children later, Chaya Malka and Yishai had relocated to the Five Towns on Long Island. Chaya Malka was quite the homemaker, baking challahs and sewing clothes for herself and her children. She also turned out to be a lovely and respectful daughter-in-law, involving Bobbi, who was now retired, in the life of her son's family. Both Chaya Malka and her children affectionately called her Bubby, the Yiddish name for grandma. Of course, Marjorie could see that Bobbi would have preferred that the children were in secular schools that followed a sound general studies curriculum. But Bobbi was a gifted enough teacher that she could sneak in lessons when she was alone with them. She was frequently in Cedarhurst, babysitting and chauffeuring the grandchildren. And she told Marjorie how she and Stanley were often invited to Friday night dinner and to sleep at Yishai's home for the Sabbath.

But the only problem was that Bobbi was not well. Marjorie knew that she had battled kidney disease for many years, but now Bobbi's nephrologist told her that her kidneys were failing and she needed to start thinking about a transplant. She confided to Marjorie that if she didn't get one, she would have to go on dialysis, which would require three to five hours of her time, three days a week.

Bobbi took Marjorie aside after synagogue services to give her the news.

"I need a kidney transplant. Although my doctor complimented me for years about the way I had made sure I ate a healthy diet and exercised, keeping my kidney disease stable, she let me know I had reached the point of no return. I knew that the test results confirmed what my body was manifesting in physical symptoms.

"I don't want to have to go on dialysis," Bobbi continued with tears in her eyes. "The survival rate after five years is only twenty-eight percent."

"How hard is it to get a transplant?"

"It's not easy," Bobbi replied.

"How do you get one?"

"The best way is to get someone in your family to donate. But my husband isn't a match and my kids have my genes. And there's no way I'm asking any of the in-laws."

"So what are you going to do?"

"Yishai told me about Renewal, an organization in Brooklyn that helps you find a kidney. It was founded by Hassidic Jews, and apparently Hassidic Jews donate their kidneys in larger numbers than any other group. So I'm going to try to see if they can find me a match."

A month later, Renewal called Bobbi to say that a match had been found and the donor wanted to schedule the transplant in three months. Bobbi thought it seemed too good to be true—and it was. After undergoing a battery of pre-op tests, she was cleared for the operation. But her joy was short-lived. She was informed by the transplant team that the donor had backed out.

Adding to Bobbi's hopelessness, her cousin Richard, who had been on dialysis for five years, died. But shortly after that, Renewal informed Bobbi that another anonymous altruistic donor had stepped up to the plate. Wary of her prior experience,

Bobbi didn't want to tell anyone—except her children—until the surgery was over. They were all happy and relieved, but Yishai and Chaya Malka were absolutely giddy.

The morning the transplant was to take place, Bobbi was in a hospital bed chatting with her husband and a representative from Renewal, who were in the room with her. Suddenly, Yishai walked into the room with a broad smile on his face.

"*Boker tov,*" he said as he walked over to his mother and gave her a big hug. "I thought you could use some company."

Rabbi Menachem Zeitlin, the Renewal representative, rose to shake hands with him.

"Your son's timing is perfect," Rabbi Zeitlin said to Bobbi. "The donor is here and is excited to be doing this mitzvah. She wants to FaceTime you."

"I thought the donor was anonymous," Bobbi said.

"Only if they want to be," Rabbi Zeitlin said.

He handed Bobbi his cell phone and there in a surgical gown, hooked up to an IV, was her daughter-in-law, Chaya Malka.

"What's this? What are you doing in the hospital? Are you all right?"

"I'm fine, Bubby. I'm giving you my kidney."

Bobbi was dumbfounded and for a moment speechless, but then she recovered. "But why?"

"Because it's a mitzvah, and you're my other mother and I want my children to have their Bubby for a long time."

And then they prayed together, saying the Shehecheyanu, a prayer of thanksgiving, in Hebrew and in English. *Blessed are You, our God, Sovereign of all, who has kept us in life, sustained us, and brought us to this moment.*

Bobbi made a mental note that she would have to tell Marjorie that she wanted to take back everything—the stereotypes, the misconceptions, and the prejudices she had held against a branch of her own people. Bobbi was in awe of her daughter-in-law's kindness and generosity.

A half hour later, Bobbi was wheeled into the operating room. Several hours later, the doctor came out to the surgical waiting room and told Stanley and Yishai that the surgery was complete and went well. Both Bobbi and Chaya Malka were resting comfortably.

The next day Chaya Malka, who was dressed to leave the hospital, walked into Bobbi's room and they embraced with tears in their eyes.

Bobbi was so touched by this gift of life from her daughter-in-law. By giving her kidney, Chaya Malka had not only rescued her from pain and suffering but also given her a new lease on life. What greater mitzvah could there be—a second chance to watch the family grow, to be productive, to breathe freely, to live.

19

Never Again

Marjorie and Leah met and became good friends on a study tour of Europe after their junior year of college. As a student at Queens College in 1969, Marjorie enjoyed being away from home for the entire summer, even staying in some college dorms. At the University of London, Marjorie and Leah and the rest of the thirty students in their group each had their own sparse and spartan single room with a twin bed, desk, and chest of drawers. There was a communal bathroom on the floor, and the first time Marjorie got up in the middle of the night to use the restroom, she was shocked to see a male student heading there. She waited for him to come out before going in.

Marjorie and Leah, both of whom were Jewish, bonded with Patty, an Irish-Catholic girl who played the guitar. Each evening the three girls would crowd into Patty's room with three male students—Vivek, an Indian, was studying air conditioning and refrigeration; Sunil, from Ceylon, was a smiling, brown-faced boy who played the sitar; and Dev, who was half Indian and half Arab, hailed from Uganda. He was a doctoral student, and Marjorie enjoyed the philosophical conversations they had when they weren't singing "Leaving on a Jet Plane" while Patty accompanied them on her guitar. The girls would give the boys their kidney pies and other strange foods they refused to eat themselves in the school cafeteria, and that's how these spoiled American girls bonded with these boys from developing nations.

All of them agreed that the war in Vietnam was unjust and the United States ought to withdraw immediately. The only source of real disagreement was the Six-Day War, which had been won by Israel in lightning speed two years earlier.

"I think Israel should give back the land it took," said Dev.

"I think they will give up all but Jerusalem," said Marjorie. "The rest of the land is just a bargaining chip."

But this was all discussed in very good humor, overlooking obvious and not-so-obvious differences.

Vivek, the Indian, had been pressing Marjorie to meet him at a pub for a drink. She was not the adventurous type, but Leah was and urged her to go. "I'll go with you. Let's just check it out."

"But he's not Jewish," said Marjorie.

"He's a Hindu, but Dev is a Muslim, and I know you'd meet him in a heartbeat. Besides, maybe we'll meet some Jewish guys there; there are a lot of British Jews, or maybe some American students."

Marjorie agreed and they headed to the pub.

She felt liberated. She had been so sheltered by her parents, who wouldn't let her go away to college and insisted that she date only Jewish guys.

The pub was dark and filled with smoke, and Vivek smiled broadly when he saw them.

"Now what would you ladies like to drink?"

Leah asked for white wine and Marjorie, not especially accustomed to drinking, ordered the same.

They sat at a small table in the corner and Marjorie began interviewing Vivek about studying air conditioning and refrigeration in London. He indicated that when he finished his degree program he would be bringing invaluable expertise back to his home country. Cooling was in its infancy in India. Marjorie secretly thought London was not the best place to study this subject—you could barely get an ice cube there.

Vivek quickly turned his attention to Marjorie.

"I'm trying to figure out what you are," he said. "Are you French, or perhaps Italian with your dark hair and eyes?"

"No," said Marjorie, "I'm an American."

"But I mean what are you—your ethnicity?"

"I'm Jewish."

He gasped as a look of pure shock flooded his face.

"You're a Jew. You don't look like a Jew. You don't act like a Jew."

Color drained from her face and she was speechless. Now Marjorie was the one who was shocked.

"I'm Jewish too," offered Leah.

"But you look and act like a Jew," said Vivek.

"What do you mean by *that?*" Leah asked.

"Well, your nose, you know what they say about Jewish noses, and you're kind of pushy. But Marjorie, I never imagined *she* was a Jew."

Both girls sat there stunned.

"Well, she is," said Leah finally. "And we have to leave now; thanks for the drinks."

Marjorie had been trained by her mother to be polite. Part of her thought it was rude to run out after he had bought the wine for them. But Leah assured her that it would have been wrong to sit with such an antisemitic person for another minute.

The girls left the pub shaken. Marjorie was not used to drinking and she felt a little lightheaded, but Leah attended overnight college and she was used to keg parties and sipping wine.

"You can't say he didn't mean it," Leah argued. "He may have been shocked that you're Jewish because in his eyes, you don't look like one. But what he said to me was downright hateful."

"I guess you're right." Marjorie shrugged, thinking about what would happen to their cozy little circle of friends in the dorm.

"Can you believe it?" Marjorie said in a shaky voice.

"Yes, I can," said Leah. "That's why I'm making aliyah just as soon as I graduate from college. You should come with me."

"Oh, my parents would be devastated. I could never leave them."

"Well, you know," said Leah, "my father was in a concentration camp, and he lost his first wife and baby girl. Both of my parents are very supportive and may even move to Israel themselves."

"Wow," said Marjorie. "My father never wants to go anywhere. And my mother gets nervous about flying, even taking a plane to Florida. I could see that when our flight to Europe was delayed seven hours, she was a wreck. I'm actually surprised she didn't try to stop me from going to Europe. She never wanted to fly when my brother and I were kids. She used to say, *I have a responsibility to my children*. She once took a train to Canada. Can you imagine? No wonder I'm a nervous flyer. But I was determined to see Europe, so I worked part-time and saved the money myself, so I guess she didn't have a choice. After all, she joined the army when she was in her early twenties; she couldn't lock me in a closet."

After college, Leah indeed made aliyah, working for a year on a kibbutz and then moving to Tel Aviv, where she met and married an Israeli. Marjorie got a job for a company in Manhattan, thinking that she didn't really want to utilize her teaching degree right away. Most of all, she thought she might meet some nice young man in the corporate world.

Although she worked very hard, she had the vague idea that the powers that be weren't as thrilled with her as they were with Kathleen McGuire, a redhead of about the same age. Marjorie ignored the obvious favoritism and tried to do the best job she could. Marjorie's job involved constant typing. She was a good typist, sixty words a minute. But Kathleen was often on the phone with clients, and the bosses sent her out to various events. They even included Kathleen in their meetings and lunches, while Marjorie ate at her desk.

One day, Marjorie walked by the boss's office and the door was open. She heard loud laughing, and one of the head honchos was disparaging a client in a mocking voice.

"Esther Blatt is coming in at two o'clock today. Esther Blatt is so ugly and fat," he said in a singsong way. "The loud, bleached-blond dame with the hooked nose. Probably wants to Jew us down on the price."

Perhaps that's what was going on here, Marjorie thought. Was it possible that they preferred Kathleen because she was Christian, and she, Marjorie, was simply not one of them? Was she being discriminated against because she was Jewish? She discussed it with her parents when she got home.

"Antisemites," her father said. "You don't even like the job. What are you doing there?"

Her mother, always waving the flag for a career in teaching, said, "You have a degree; you're a teacher. That's what you should do."

Marjorie had to agree that this corporate world was not for her. She would get a teaching job in the fall.

During her many years as a classroom teacher, Marjorie never felt any antisemitism. After all, her principals were mostly Jewish, as were many of the teachers. And in those years it was all about racism: hiring Black people, teaching about Black history, being inclusive. Marjorie never felt that she was part of the minority.

She and her husband were active in their synagogue, supported other minority groups, and sent their kids to a Jewish day school and then on to colleges with sizeable Jewish populations. They had gone to Washington, DC, to the big march on behalf of Soviet Jews in 1987. As a small child, Marjorie's grandfather had escaped to America with his family from Kiev. But he barely remembered ever living in Russia. Occasionally, someone painted a swastika on a synagogue, but the County Police Task Force on Discrimination handled it quickly. Nevertheless, Marjorie had an aversion to wearing religious symbols in public.

"Take off your yarmulke," Marjorie said to her husband for what felt to her like the eighteen thousandth time in the course of their fifty-year-relationship. "You can't drive on the Long Island Expressway in broad daylight wearing a kippah."

He looked at her with the innocent look of a wounded child, as if he had never heard that warning from her before.

He liked wearing his yarmulke and had taken to wearing it more frequently ever since he retired, went to minyan every morning, recovered from open-heart surgery, and now had a group of male buddies. Their daughter, Deborah, had speculated that the kippah and the davening were both comforting for him.

For many years, he had only a couple of friends he kept from college and some acquaintances from the shul. Marjorie was the one with a cadre of friends, and she and Eric socialized and interacted with her friends and their partners.

But now that Eric was retired, much of his spare time revolved around his minyan friends. Like most Jews, Eric and his pals made their own rules, heading for the diner for breakfast each Friday morning after services. For the diner, he covered the kippah with a baseball cap and then brought the leftover pancakes for Marjorie to eat on a paper plate in their kosher home.

But even when he would go outside in the evening to take out the garbage cans, Marjorie would yell: "Take your kippah off!"

Eric would roll his eyes and sometimes take it off, but usually not, retorting: "You're nuts, it's dark outside, and this is a gated community with many Jews."

Marjorie herself didn't wear religious symbols throughout her childhood and young adulthood, although she became increasingly observant as she got older. She began to realize that she might have been influenced by her mother. Alice's fears were a function of having grown up during Hitler's rise to power and coming of age during World War II. Wearing a Jewish star was pejorative for that generation. Alice had shared with Marjorie an experience she had when she was twelve years old right after she moved to New Jersey from

Brooklyn. In Brooklyn all the kids were Jewish, but her new best friend in Jersey, Donna, was Catholic.

"You killed Jesus!" Donna blurted out one June day in the schoolyard. Alice was taken aback by the genuine anger in her voice and face. By this time the two girls had been inseparable for four months.

"No, I didn't," Alice shouted back, shocked at the accusation. "I didn't even know Jesus. I had nothing to do with it," Alice cried out on the verge of tears. "Why are you saying such a thing? It was so many years ago, I wasn't even alive then."

"They told me in Sunday School that the Jews killed Jesus, and you're Jewish, so you killed him."

"You're wrong. The Jews didn't kill him. It was the Romans and I know that for a fact."

"Are you sure?"

"I'm positive. Believe me. The Jews didn't kill him, and I had nothing to do with it."

"Okay. If you say so," said Donna. "Let's go to the library."

The first time they visited Jerusalem together, Eric, happily wearing his kippah, took Marjorie to Baltinester's Judaica store on Jaffa Street and bought her a filigreed gold *hamsa* with aquamarine and amethyst stones. Marjorie knew that Eric believed they had an obligation to help the Israeli economy when they were there, and as soon as she commented on how beautiful it was, before she knew it, he had purchased it for her. She felt she had no choice but to put it on immediately and wear it throughout the rest of the trip. She felt comfortable wearing it in Israel. She got many compliments on it and decided not to take it off when she returned home to Long Island. When she secretly convinced herself that it wasn't as blatant as a Jewish star, she realized that she had inherited not only her mother's fear of flying but also her anxiety about antisemites.

Marjorie continued to work on her fear of flying, but she was still not convinced that antisemitism wasn't a threat to her or her family in the United States. She had experienced overt antisemitism only twice in her lifetime, both when she was barely out of adolescence.

I am being ridiculous. We live in a gated community in a Jewish neighborhood. There are four synagogues within seven miles of each other. And although the lone kosher butcher in Suffolk County has gone out of business, there is still a kosher deli, kosher food in ShopRite, and Woodbury Kosher and Ben's fifteen minutes away in Plainview.

But somehow, Marjorie was just uncomfortable with Eric wearing his yarmulke to North Shore Farms or even ShopRite.

"What's your problem with it?" he asked her.

"I feel like you're representing all of the Jewish people when you wear it. Your manners have to be impeccable; you have to give a generous tip; you can't ever get angry at anyone; you must never quibble about a price."

"That's ridiculous," he said. "If someone is wearing a cross, do you hold them to that standard?"

"Of course not," she said. "It's a Christian country."

"Well then, we should have moved to Israel when we were first married like I wanted to."

"But we weren't fluent in Hebrew."

"We could have learned."

"I never would have left my parents."

"Well, that's for sure," Eric said.

"I have to admit," said Marjorie, "when I watch i24NEWS"—an English-language broadcast from Israel—"I'm a bit wistful that we didn't go. I love Owen Alterman and Calev Ben-David, and they're Americans. They made outstanding careers for themselves in Israel. And I used to be afraid of terror attacks, but it seems so safe now."

"It's much safer than it used to be," Eric said. "I could have easily been a doctor in Israel, but what's the point? I'm seventy-five now."

And then in the early hours of October 7, 2023, the whole world changed—not only for Marjorie and Eric, but for all Jews in Israel and around the world.

Their son Josh called them, waking them up with the news: "Israel is at war!"

They switched on i24, and there was the anchor Ellie Hochenberg, with her expressive face and voice and unruly head of brown curls, reporting from Israel about the unspeakable horrors that Hamas had rained on innocent Jews sleeping in their beds. It was a quiet Shabbat morning that was also the Jewish holiday of Simchat Torah.

Marjorie knew deep in her heart that the world would soon shift from support for Israel because of the unprovoked surprise attack by Hamas to sympathy for the Palestinians of Gaza who had elected Hamas as their leaders. That's the way it always turned out for Israel, who for all of its innovations had never mastered public relations.

She feared public opinion would soon forget the rapes, the beheadings, the torture, the kidnapping of 253 innocent people, and the slaughtering of 1,200 innocent Jews.

In November, she rejoiced in the release of 112 of the

hostages, but her heart continued to break for those still in captivity, especially for the youngest, Kfir Bibas, an adorable redheaded baby.

When Israel went to war with Hamas, Marjorie added Leah and her husband, children, and grandchildren to her prayers. Leah's grandson and granddaughter were on active duty in the Israel Defense Forces. Leah told her that everyone she knew was somehow touched by the war. Not a day went by when there wasn't a funeral among her friends, relatives, and acquaintances. Business as usual had come to a halt.

It took but a few weeks, and Marjorie and Jews throughout the world began to understand the fears her mother and Jews of her generation had carried in their hearts for their entire lives.

But unlike her mother, Marjorie searched in her jewelry box for the Star of David her grandmother Sadie had given her. She put it around her neck, along with the *hamsa*. She even tried to stop herself from telling Eric to remove his yarmulke when he took out the garbage. A few weeks later, both Marjorie and her husband bought "Bring Them Home—Now" hostage dog tags. And on Shabbat, along with the entire congregation, they faced the back of the sanctuary where a poster of each hostage was affixed to a chair. They prayed for their increasingly unlikely safe return.

Six months later, as Marjorie and her family were about to sit down for the first Seder at her house, there was a knock on the door.

"Is anyone expecting someone?" she called out, and there was a loud chorus of no.

"Okay, I'll get it," she said as she walked to the front door.

She opened it and was startled to see her eighteen-year-old grandson, Joseph, standing there, breathless with an agonized look on his face.

"What's the matter, Joey? What happened?" she asked as she hugged him.

"You wouldn't believe what's going on at my college. I took the train from Manhattan. Palestinian protesters have taken over the campus and kicked out the Jews. They've set up a tent city, and even if you're not Jewish, but have Jewish friends, they're targeting you. They seem to know who all the Jewish students are; it's as if they have radar. They ordered me to get off the campus, and the rabbi told us to leave for our own safety. Classes will be online for the rest of the semester. So I came here."

With tears in her eyes, Marjorie continued to embrace him as she thought about the irony of this year's Seder. They would observe the festival of freedom—as more than 130 innocent hostages languished or worse in Gaza, and antisemitic profanity was being hurled at her grandson and his Jewish classmates. These attacks on blameless Jewish college students evoked memories not only of Jewish enslavement millennia ago in Egypt, but of her parents, who had fought against the Nazis in World War II. And of Leah's father, who was a Holocaust survivor. Wasn't this how it had all started in Germany in the 1930s?

Where was the world when Jews were in peril? Marjorie had lived nearly three-quarters of a century mostly in a cocoon, feeling free and safe. But so had the Jews of Germany.

She grabbed a folding chair and quickly set another place for Joey at the beautifully set Seder table. She admired the ornate Seder plate from Israel with the symbols of the holiday, and the matzah and the wine. At each place there was a little glass dish with salt water, a hard-boiled egg, and parsley. Luckily she had boiled extra eggs. She went to the refrigerator and put one in the bowl at Joseph's place.

Scents of chicken and chicken soup and potato kugel filled the kitchen, but the dining room smelled of eggs representing the circle of life. The egg was a symbol of renewal and hope even in the most trying times.

Passover had always been Marjorie's favorite holiday, ever since she was a small child. She normally prepared for the holiday with joy—scouring the kitchen, bringing out the Passover dishes, shopping for kosher Passover items, and preparing the special dishes. But this was a most unusual Passover, and she was not joyful. But she knew that every Jew in every generation was obligated to celebrate the holiday, observing the festival of freedom, even in troubling times. She had read that Jews had even tried to observe it in the ghettos and concentration camps. There were prayers in the Haggadah specially written for those in captivity who did not have matzah for the holiday.

She took a deep breath, glad that her family was together and that Joey was safe. And she would try her hardest as they proceeded with the Seder to repress her indignation at the student protesters. What had higher education come to? In her day, there was fierce disagreement about the war in Vietnam. But students had not threatened other students. They hashed out their differences in teach-ins, where both sides were presented and argued.

The Seder rituals felt different, wrong for this moment in time. How would they joyfully and boisterously sing

"Dayenu" this year? "Dayenu," meaning "it would have been enough," had always been her family's favorite Seder song. Sung to an uplifting tune, it lists the miracles God performed for the Jewish people during and after the Exodus. Her family was so distracted and distraught about Joey's experience, they actually forgot to sing it.

After all the guests were gone and Marjorie stood at the kitchen sink washing the eighteen wineglasses by hand, she thought about the campus protests and the chants borne of ignorance and hatred. Sighing to herself, she wondered if these young people even understood what they were chanting. Did they know which river and which sea they were talking about? Were they okay with the mass murders, rapes, and atrocities committed on October 7?

And then a wineglass slipped from her hand and shattered on the floor.

As she bent down to pick up the pieces, she cut her finger, and the blood began to flow.

The house was still. There was no one to talk to; everyone had gone home and Eric was asleep in their king-size bed. He could sleep through anything.

Marjorie began to scream—a woeful wail of pain and indignation—for centuries of prejudice, antisemitism, and misunderstanding, which had now come to her grandson's campus and to her Seder. Was *Never Again* now?

She thought of the very last words of the Haggadah, *Next Year in Jerusalem,* which Jews had recited for millennia. She washed her hands and put a Band-Aid on her finger. As she collapsed onto the bed, she thought of Leah and all the other American Jews who had made aliyah. She uttered a prayer for them—and for the Sabras, for the children of Holocaust survivors, for the Ethiopians, the Russians, the Moroccans, the Yemenites, the Druze, the Christians, the Arabs, and all the others who made up the melting pot that was Israel. She prayed also for the innocent Palestinian children, whom Hamas deliberately placed in the middle of the conflict. And for her grandson and all the Jewish students on college campuses. She would have to call Joey in the morning and remind him not to wear his yarmulke in public.

20

Virtual Daughter

The last public event Marjorie and Eric attended before the COVID-19 shutdown was the synagogue's Purim party. Costumes were optional, and Eric donned Nigerian formal attire, which consisted of a three-piece red-and-gold set. It had an open-stitched full gown, a long-sleeved shirt, and trousers fitted snugly at the ankle. It had been loaned to him by Micah Nussbaum, who in traveling to the African country on business had adopted a group of people who identified as Jews. He collected prayer books and prayer shawls and periodically conducted services for them when he was there.

Marjorie was aware of the COVID shutdown in New Rochelle. As a result, she was not convinced that they should even attend this Purim gala, but Eric persuaded her, anxious to wear the costume. She reluctantly went along, although she did not wear a costume.

It was a lively event held in the synagogue ballroom with a DJ and hummus, pita and falafel, and desserts served buffet-style.

Marjorie's author friend Cynthia Levy, who was not in costume either, commented that perhaps the event should have been cancelled.

"I agree," said Marjorie. "I told Eric that we shouldn't go. I know Bonnie Morrison from Camp Ramah. She lives in New Rochelle, and the whole community was shut down. This is scary. But you know how insistent Bobbi is. She organized the whole thing, and she kept calling me to make sure we would show up."

"It's a big fundraiser for the shul; that's Bobbi's bottom line," Cynthia said as they stood in the middle of the dance floor while couples whizzed by in costume dressed as the popular figures of the Purim story—Queen Esther, the king, Mordecai, and the evil Haman. There were even a few hamantaschen—three-sided pastry with fruit filling. Cynthia wore a tiara and a business suit. She was standing so close to Marjorie that she grabbed her hand and Marjorie could feel her breath on her face.

"Do you think it's safe to eat?" Marjorie asked. She hadn't eaten dinner and was hungry.

"I guess so," Cynthia replied. "Let's get something."

The whole way home in the car, Marjorie lamented to Eric that they shouldn't have gone.

"How do I get your friends to stop kissing me hello? It's bad enough that we exposed ourselves in a crowd tonight, but can you believe that Jack Wolinsky tried—as usual—to kiss me on the mouth? He's such a lech."

"He's an old guy; he loves you."

"Ugh. And I kept running to the Purell sanitizer dispenser; my hands are going to be chapped. You know I also never felt comfortable with all the handshaking, let alone the kissing at shul. Maybe this will finally put an end to it."

By the following weekend, the whole country had shut down. Marjorie read in the Jewish newspaper that an acquaintance had dropped dead in his living room on Shabbat after only a week of COVID; a week later, a neighbor two doors down also died from the virus.

At first Marjorie didn't mind the lockdown. She signed up for an Instacart account and enjoyed the luxury of having her groceries delivered to their front door. She tried to hoard toilet paper, paper towels, and hand sanitizer in case one of her kids, whom she had not seen since the shutdown, needed it. She ended up sending a case of toilet paper to her son in Arizona, who couldn't find it on the shelves or online. She couldn't see her grandchildren, who were now "going to school" on Zoom. As a parent and educator, she cried—especially for the two kindergartners who were being especially shortchanged.

Because it was essential if she wanted any human contact, Marjorie learned how to communicate by FaceTime and Zoom. Still, she was relieved that she had retired from her teaching job. Luckily Eric had also retired from medicine a couple of years earlier due to a heart condition, so there was no risk of him getting COVID in the hospital.

But when Passover was suddenly around the corner, the weeks of quarantine had already turned into a month. Marjorie just couldn't imagine a Zoom Seder. Since she was a child, the joy was sitting at the Seder table with all of her quirky relatives, taking turns reading the Haggadah, smelling the special foods, and enjoying the meal together. But now, like everything else, the unthinkable had become real. The upside was that she didn't have to prepare a Seder for twenty people, and her family that was now spread out throughout the country would be able to gather together for the first time in years. The downside was that her children and grandchildren and brother and sister-in-law and nephews and nieces were all reduced to little squares. How she longed to embrace her children and grandchildren. There would be no little kids gleefully running around her house trying to find the afikomen this year.

After Passover, Cynthia told Marjorie that she needed to be on Facebook. It was the place to be if she wanted to socialize with like-minded people. There were so many wonderful groups, she said. Cynthia had "met" other authors with whom she could discuss common issues, and she was building up a cadre of readers—people who would read and review her books. She recommended that Marjorie join a book club too, so she did.

Before the pandemic, Marjorie had been in the habit of reading a book for the Sisterhood Book Club, which met once a month. But now with little to do, she began reading in earnest. After joining Bethany's Book Club, she found herself commenting on the Facebook site and posting about books she was reading.

Whenever she posted, another member named Catelyn wrote a comment about the book she was referencing and then added another recommended book in return. Marjorie, of course, always polite and appreciative of responses, answered her each time. It wasn't long before Facebook posts gave her the sense of playing the slot machines in a casino. Years ago she had enjoyed a physical rush when she won but eventually decided she was in danger of following in the footsteps of her great-uncle, who was a gambler. His first wife divorced him because she eventually found herself in an apartment with no furniture because of his debts.

But Facebook was another matter, Marjorie reasoned. It didn't cost anything and, heck, there was a pandemic going on. She was making virtual friends, and she was reading lots of books. She soon became one of the top contributors to the book club, and some of the members sent her friend requests.

One of these new "friends" was Catelyn, who frequently posted about her work-in-progress, which she said she had been working on for four years. One day Marjorie realized that the little cloud with a number on it meant she had a message.

"You're so perceptive and sensitive," Catelyn wrote. "I can tell by your comments. Can I send you a chapter of my book to read?"

"Of course, I'd love to," Marjorie wrote back. "I'm so flattered and honored."

Catelyn asked her for her cell number and email, and Marjorie complied right away.

But instead of sending her the chapter, Catelyn called her on the phone.

"I'm just polishing up the chapter before I send it to you, but I'm so depressed. I have no one to talk to." Catelyn started right in as if they were already real friends.

"Do you live alone, Catelyn?"

"No, I live with my husband, but he's hardly ever home and he doesn't talk to me," Catelyn replied as she started to cry. "I feel so alone. I'm by myself all day and I have no one to talk to. My sister is mad at me, and my mother is siding with her. No one loves me."

"Don't cry," Marjorie said. "It can't be that bad. You're writing a book, so why don't you concentrate on that and get it done? I'd love to read that chapter when you're ready to send it."

"Thank you, I will. You're so soothing to talk to. Is it all right if I call you again?"

"Of course," said Marjorie.

Catelyn began texting Marjorie and calling her often. Marjorie learned that Catelyn was thirty-seven. Her texts were always about her perceived injuries. Her mother hated her. Her sister was sneaky. A friend had abandoned her. She had blocked another Facebook friend because she had insulted her.

Marjorie listened attentively, always trying to be soothing and positive, but she was also aware that she was spending more time talking to Catelyn than to her own children.

One day Catelyn called convinced she had COVID. "I'm coughing and I have a fever, and Jim just doesn't care. He'd probably be happy if I died."

"Don't say that, Catelyn," Marjorie said. "I'm sure he cares. But you must test yourself for COVID. Will you promise me you'll do that?"

"We don't have any test kits here."

"Well, tell Jim he needs to get some. It's a matter of life and death."

In the meantime, Marjorie went online and ordered chicken soup and a chicken dinner, which she had delivered to Catelyn's home.

Catelyn tested negative for COVID. But her complaints and the calls to Marjorie escalated.

One morning at 5:30 a.m., Catelyn texted. The ding awakened Eric.

"What's wrong?" he said. "Which kid is it?"

"Our kids aren't up at this hour. It's Catelyn," Marjorie said as she read the text on her cell phone.

Eric groaned and went back to sleep.

"Call me," Catelyn wrote. "I can't breathe."

Marjorie took the phone into the kitchen, sat down at the table, and dialed Catelyn.

"What do you mean you can't breathe?"

"I think I'm having a heart attack."

"Where's Jim?"

"He's sleeping. Eric is a doctor. Can't you ask him what I should do?"

Marjorie went back into the bedroom, woke Eric up, and asked what Catelyn should do.

"She should go to the hospital," he said.

Marjorie relayed the message to Catelyn. When Catelyn called her back hours later, she informed Marjorie that she hadn't gone to the hospital; Jim had said it was too dangerous with COVID raging.

After that, Catelyn began to call every day with a new health concern. She complained that her husband either ignored her or yelled at her. At least once a week, she told Marjorie that someone posted something insulting about her on Facebook and she said she was going to block them. Her family had abandoned her. She cried to Marjorie that she had no money. Most of all, she said over and over again that Marjorie was the only one who understood her. In response, Marjorie sent her a basket of goodies to cheer her up.

"How can you love someone you've never met?" Eric asked. "I think the lockdown has clouded your reason—you need a project that's not Catelyn. It's clear to me that since you can't do your usual volunteer work, she's become your project. I think you worry about her more than you do about our kids."

"Our kids are not as needy as she is; they're functioning in this awful situation."

Eric shook his head.

Months went by. Weddings, bar and bat mitzvahs, birthday and anniversary parties were cancelled or held on Zoom.

One morning, Catelyn sent a text that it was urgent for Marjorie to call her. She told Marjorie she didn't have any money.

"They cut Jim's salary. I'm afraid they'll turn off our electricity. Can you loan me some cash? I'll pay you back. I promise," she cried hysterically on the phone.

"How much do you need?"

"About $200."

"No problem. How should I send it to you?"

"Venmo," she replied instantly.

Within minutes, the money was sent.

"Happy Hanukkah," Catelyn chirped on the first day of the holiday several weeks later. "I wish I could afford to buy you a present."

"Oh, that's not necessary."

"I love you, Mom. I'm writing a poem for you."

Marjorie wondered if she was hearing correctly. Had Catelyn just called her "Mom"?

"That's so sweet," she said, ignoring the possibility. Instead she focused on the poem. Marjorie had framed the poem her son Seth had written for her when he was in high school. It still touched her heart. Now, Marjorie began in earnest to think of what she should get Catelyn for Christmas—a person who thought enough of her to write her a poem.

"What would you like for Christmas?" she asked.

"Honestly, Marjorie. You don't have to get me anything. You're my Jewish mom."

This time there was no denying it, so Marjorie thought she might as well play along.

"But mothers always get their children presents."

"Nothing frivolous, please. We're still having trouble paying our bills."

Marjorie mailed a Christmas card with a check for $360 a few days before the holiday.

"This will come in handy," said Catelyn. "We're not invited to my mother's for Christmas. My sister has turned her against me, so we'll be making our own dinner. And we'll use the rest to pay our bills. Because of the pandemic, Jim isn't getting his usual bonus this year," Catelyn said in the way of thank you.

"Oh, I'm so sorry to hear that, Catelyn. But you know the number 360 is symbolic. In the Jewish religion, 18 stands for *chai,* which means life. So 360 is 20 times 18; it's a wish for life and health."

"That's so sweet, Marjorie. I love you, Mom, and I love Eric too."

Catelyn had never met or spoken to Eric or seen his face. How could she love him? Maybe she thought she loved him because the gift was from him too—which it wasn't. While Eric was charitable, Marjorie had a feeling that he would not approve.

The two women went on like this for years, during which Marjorie sent many gifts and donations that were not reciprocated. Finally, when the pandemic was over, Catelyn called with good news.

"I'm having a fortieth birthday party," she said. "Please come and bring Eric too."

Marjorie assumed it would be an intimate affair since Catelyn was estranged from most of her family and had few friends. Still, she was excited about the prospect of meeting Catelyn in person. How wonderful it would be to meet this young woman who called her "Mom." She was actually relieved that Eric had no interest in attending. There might not be anyone for him to talk to.

Marjorie also had to think of the perfect gift. She scoured the listings on Etsy and found a Swarovski crystal friendship necklace. She bought a heartfelt and flowery birthday card. But then remembering how strapped Catelyn always was for cash, she decided to add a check representative of her age—forty times ten—$400.

The day of the party Marjorie put on a pair of black slacks, a white top, and a royal-blue blazer with a matching scarf. Her hair was freshly colored and coiffed. Catelyn's party was being held in the party room of the condo in which she and Jim lived, a mere forty-five minutes from Marjorie's home.

She found the condo easily and an attendant parked her car for her. Marjorie had expected a more modest edifice, certainly not one where they parked your car for you. The building itself had a luxurious quality to it with a large chandelier, fireplace, and modern white-leather furniture in the lobby.

When she entered the party room, Marjorie was surprised to see about seventy-five well-dressed, well-coiffed women and a handful of men. This had not been the small and motley group of people she had expected. She had thought that someone who was about to lose their electricity would have a less affluent-looking group of friends. And while there were a few people Catelyn's age, many were quite a bit older.

The party room was lovely with eight tables, set with pink tablecloths and pastel balloon centerpieces. In the front of the room, a DJ was playing. At the left side of the room were two tables, a small one with a pink and white sheet cake that said *Happy 40th Birthday Catelyn.* Next to it was another long table laden with cheese and crackers, chips and dips, and a charcuterie platter.

There was a long table in the back of the room piled high with wrapped gift boxes, gift bags, and a box for envelopes—ostensibly for cash gifts.

As Marjorie placed her gift bag on the table, she spotted Catelyn. She had pictured the actual meeting as a coming together in person of two souls who had become attached to each other before they ever met. She had imagined the joyful embrace of two individuals who were so special to each other.

In person Catelyn was skinny, bordering on anorexia, with bleached-blond hair and green eyes. She wore a short pink lace dress and white leather boots, none of which looked inexpensive to Marjorie's eyes.

Seated on a peacock chair, Catelyn held court. Guests greeted her and took her hand, some kissed her on the cheek, but Catelyn never changed her expression. Her green eyes looked cold, and a smile was frozen on her face. The chair was made of white wicker with a dramatic, highly arched back, which fanned out like a peacock's tail. It was decorated with pink ribbons and bows. Marjorie had seen these chairs at weddings and showers, but never at a forty-year-old's birthday party.

Marjorie took a place at the end of the line of people waiting to greet the birthday girl. *Who were these friends of Catelyn?*

she wondered. This was not the party of a person whose electricity was in danger of being shut off at any minute. As she stood there waiting her turn, she chastised herself for thinking Catelyn and her husband didn't have enough to eat.

Marjorie wondered if Catelyn called all of her friends "Mom."

As she waited on the line, Marjorie watched Catelyn as she extended her hand to her guests, some shaking it, others kissing it, and still others leaning in and kissing her cheek. And while she smiled, her expression never varied. Catelyn's green eyes were cold and steely.

As Marjorie finally stepped forward, she expected a special reaction from her online daughter. She had imagined that she was unique to Catelyn, her second "mom." She was sure she would get a different greeting than those who had been ahead of her in the line.

She was about to open her arms, but Catelyn simply extended her hand and greeted her with a cold peck on the cheek. She said nothing more and quickly turned to greet the next person in line.

Marjorie truly felt as if she had been smacked, and she fought to hold back tears. She had convinced herself that she loved Catelyn. After all, didn't Catelyn say that she loved her? She had believed that the young woman had been abandoned by her mother. But her mother was there, one of the few guests who spoke to Marjorie. And Jim? Although you never know what goes on in someone else's home, he appeared to be okay. She wondered if he had been part of the swindle too.

While Marjorie was open-hearted and charitable, never before had she felt scammed. She had never regretted a penny she had given away—to a reputable charity, a GoFundMe page, or a homeless person on the street. It wasn't the money, but the deception, the lying, and of course, her own naïveté that bothered her now. She wondered if the rest of the guests were also victims of Catelyn's manipulation. *Probably so,* she thought.

She wondered, *If your eyes are indeed mirrors of your soul, was it possible to truly know someone you had not met in person?*

Obviously, she realized, it was impossible. She began to hyperventilate, and she was afraid she would throw up. Yes, she was stunned, and she knew that she had been duped. She understood that her virtual daughter was nothing more than a con artist and a queen of online manipulation.

Furious with herself for being so gullible, she rushed across the room, grabbed her present from the gift table, and turned and left the party.

21

Celebrity

Marjorie's original exposure to cable TV happened in the eighties when pay TV first came to her neighborhood. As she sat cuddling her baby for the 2:00 a.m. feeding, it was comforting to have CNN as company. Now forty years later, the war between the United Kingdom and Argentina that took place that year had been largely forgotten by the world. But in those ensuing years, Marjorie had learned the wonders of endless TV.

She was old enough to remember a faraway time when TV stations would go off the air with the flying of the American flag, accompanied by the playing of "The Star-Spangled Banner." But ever since Marjorie sat in the darkness with her newborn and soaked up the seventy-four days of the Falklands War, she had become addicted to the names and faces on twenty-four-hour cable TV.

A highlight was in 1991, when she first began to rely upon Wolf Blitzer during the first Gulf War. A former Washington correspondent for the *Jerusalem Post,* it was rumored that he took the job at the fledgling station for $45,000 a year. At first, comedians made fun of his unusual name. But now, well into his seventies and still going strong, he had become an icon.

Over the years, as TV screens became larger and larger, Marjorie became more of a cable TV addict. She flipped the channels so she could see the different takes on breaking news. The life-size TV personalities were so persistently and pervasively in their den, kitchen, and bedroom that Eric suggested, "Why don't you just invite them in for coffee?"

She secretly wished she could, especially because she knew the names and faces of all the reporters and pundits and felt like they were important people in her life. She certainly relied on what she believed to be their informed, erudite, and well-researched opinions—especially when she agreed with them.

As she watched and listened carefully to the many commentators on her big screen who interpreted the news of the day, she hung on their every word. She conflated the fact that they were articulate, good-looking, and well-groomed with their skills of prophecy and analysis. So, if a pundit said something that Marjorie was thinking, she would excitedly call her mother and say that someone on cable TV agreed with her, as if that made it true or gave it more weight by being on the tongues of these modern-day prophets. But somehow, Marjorie believed it did.

While she was teaching, Marjorie began and ended her day with cable TV. And once she retired, if she was at home, it was on all day in the background. When there was breaking news, she knew right away. She would immediately text her children. They told her she watched too much cable.

Forty years after the Falkland War, Marjorie had been watching cable TV so long, she could tell you who had had a face lift, which men had started coloring their hair, and how old every single anchor was. She also knew their place of birth, religion, and sexual orientation.

As a kid, Marjorie had started watching *Meet the Press* on NBC when JFK began running for president. And she loved the talk shows, especially David Susskind. But what she admired the most were the women on TV—Pauline Frederick at the UN back in the day and also Barbara Walters with her probing interviews. She was also intrigued by Nancy Dickerson, the trailblazing TV correspondent.

Marjorie yearned to follow in their footsteps, but not being self-confident or prescient, she didn't see the opportunities that were on the horizon for women.

Instead she took her mother Alice's advice: "Become an elementary school teacher. After you get married and have children, your hours will be the same as theirs, and you'll have the summers off and all the school holidays."

It probably would have made more sense for Marjorie to teach social studies, but she was a dutiful daughter, only later realizing that her mother wanted her to live out her dreams.

Still, she maintained her passion for politics and helped local candidates. In fact, one year she had the experience of serving as an alternate delegate at the Democratic National Convention. It was the year that Hillary Clinton was the first woman ever to secure a major party nomination.

For Marjorie, going to Philadelphia for the convention was like a child being let loose in a candy store. There she met a few of her idols, who were warm and friendly and expressed delight that she was a viewer. How exciting to meet celebrities in the flesh. Mika Brzezinski was charming and friendly, and Howard Fineman was a lovely gentleman. Paul Begala gave her a big smile when they passed in the hall.

At the convention center, she was sitting on the aisle in the bleachers and there was an empty seat next to her. She was excited to see Noah Kalkstein, a fortyish man wearing a pinstriped navy-blue suit, a white shirt, and a light blue tie. He was standing six rows down on the aisle, scanning the bleachers looking for an empty seat. She knew that his son was a classmate of one of her grandsons at a Jewish day school in Manhattan. He frequently opined on cable TV. She waved to get his attention and pointed to the empty seat next to her.

He smiled, walked up the steps, and Marjorie extended her hand.

"Hi," she said. "I'm Marjorie Grossman. My grandson Jared is friends with your son, Doron. They're in the same class at the Westside Day School."

"Sure, I know Jared. Thanks for pointing out the empty seat. It's so packed here. I'm going to be interviewed about the convention on TV in a couple of hours."

"What are you going to say?"

"I have no idea other than discussing the historic nature of the first woman in US history being nominated for president. This is going to be such a boring election. Hillary is a shoo-in to beat Donald Trump. Do you have any thoughts?"

Marjorie looked at this young man, who was about the same age as her sons. She noted to herself that all of them hadn't even been born during the Watergate scandal. For them, it was all a history lesson. And why did Noah think he had a crystal ball? Well, at least he was open-minded enough to ask her what she thought.

"Well, if I were on, I wouldn't say it's a shoo-in or a boring election," she told him. "You never know. There's still a lot of sexism out there. The campaign is not yet in full swing and there have already been openly sexist remarks made about

Hillary. Not to mention comments that would never be made of a man, such as criticizing the colors of her clothing and saying she doesn't smile enough. Worst of all, it's just tone-deaf to suggest that she should emulate male politicians."

"I hear you," Noah said. "Thanks for your thoughts, but I don't agree. Trump doesn't have a chance. You'll see, she will be elected."

When the proceedings were almost over, Marjorie left her seat to go to the restroom. In the hall she spotted Leo Spencer, one of her favorite cable hosts. He had the distinction of having been an aide to a prestigious member of Congress. She often quoted him because she trusted him and respected his opinion. She ran over to him, so excited to meet him.

She put out her hand. "Hi, Leo, I'm Marjorie Grossman from New York. I watch your show religiously. I'm a big fan. I often quote your opinions."

He gave her a limp handshake but didn't make eye contact with her. She could see he was looking around to see who else was in the hall. But there was something more she wanted to say:

"Just a friendly piece of advice," she said. "Especially now that Hillary is running for president, you might want to watch some of the comments you make about women. They could be interpreted as sexist."

"What are you saying?" he said to her in a loud voice with a sneer. "You don't know what you're talking about. Is there anything else you want to say to me?"

"No, that's it. Nice meeting you."

Stunned by his outburst, Marjorie walked away, crushed that her favorite talk show host was so rude and nasty. *I'm done with him.* When she got back to her hotel room, she turned on her laptop and googled Leo Spencer and sexism. Sure enough, a recent video of his sexist comments popped up, with references to others he had made previously. It confirmed her recollection and that others shared her belief that he had been making sexist comments.

Then she turned on the TV. There was Noah Kalkstein, pontificating about Hillary's nomination. He had not taken her advice. He said she would certainly be elected in November.

The lightbulb went off in Marjorie's head and she saw Noah for what he was—a person who was likely on TV because he was nice-looking, personable, articulate, and telegenic. His opinions were neither more nor less significant than any other knowledgeable person's. It suddenly dawned on her that he had sat next to her and watched the same speakers she had and was merely giving his opinion. She could have done the same thing.

And what about Leo Spencer? She had been watching him for years. She doubted that she would ever watch him again. Not only was he a sexist pig, but he also couldn't even take responsibility for his own words.

While she would likely not continue to watch Leo, she couldn't imagine going cold turkey from her viewing habits. She would just have to be a more discerning watcher of cable TV.

As she was beating herself up for confronting Leo, Daniel Boorstin's book *The Image* came to mind. She had read it when she was in college. Perhaps she would reread it now. She remembered his definition of *celebrity* because it hit home now. "A person who is known for his well-known-ness." Nothing more, nothing less.

22

The 103-Year-Old Woman

Marjorie turned off the TV in disgust. Her children were right: she had to cure herself of this cable TV news habit.

She would wake up to it at 6:00 a.m. and put it on again at midnight just before going to sleep to make sure nothing monumental had happened in the world.

Dominating the news now was the issue of President Joe Biden's age: whether, at the age of eighty-one, he had the cognitive ability to be president for another four years. She had been a political junkie ever since she was in junior high, and she fell in love with JFK during his campaign for president. Now with what looked like a likely rematch between two presidential candidates who were past their prime, she honestly wished they both would just go away. This had nothing to do with politics—it was the age thing.

Were they too old? Did they have the stamina? How was their physical stamina and mental acuity?

If she heard the word *elderly* one more time, she was going to scream.

While Marjorie thought both were indeed too old to shoulder the crushing responsibilities of president of the United States, she hated the conversation. Although she was a few years younger than they were, she was still a septuagenarian. But, hey, now even Oprah was.

Of course, when Marjorie turned forty and then fifty, and even sixty, popular culture had made her feel old. But now, beautiful celebrities like Salma Hayek, Vanessa Williams, and Julia Roberts were in their fifties and sixties. Sixty was considered the new forty, and Marjorie suspected that it wouldn't be until Jennifer Aniston turned seventy that it too would be considered young. Of course, by then Marjorie would be in her eighties.

She concluded that she was simply born too soon—destined to be deemed old forever. She hated the word *elderly*. It made her conjure up little old women with white hair who were bent over and old men with walkers and in wheelchairs who were unable to remember the names of their grandchildren. And she was annoyed with the media and its use of the word *elderly* to describe average people who were victimized in unfortunate accidents or attacks:

The victims of the house fire were an elderly couple (sixty-six and seventy years old)

An elderly woman crashed her car into a convenience store (sixty-three years old)

An elderly man was stabbed by a masked assailant in the park (seventy-three years old)

In contrast, Marjorie noted that they would never think of labeling one of their own journalists as elderly. Instead, they were *expert, veteran, venerable, respected, esteemed,* and *admired.*

What was old anyway?

Marjorie's grandfather Mayer had died from prostate cancer in the era before it was curable. He was only seventy-two, but he looked like an old man. She remembered the days before he was admitted to the hospital for the last time; she sat in his bedroom and sang to him, trying to drown out the moans from his excruciating pain.

After he died, Marjorie's grandmother Sadie came to live with them. Marjorie remembered her silver-gray hair rolled in curls under a hairnet and her sturdy old lady shoes—heavy leather black oxfords with laces. She took a "constitutional" every day. Everyone marveled at how amazing she was for seventy and, indeed, she was still impressive when she passed away at ninety-two with all of her faculties, including her strong opinions. Marjorie shuddered to think that she was already five years older than her grandmother had been when she came to live with them. But there were many Sadies nowadays. There were even nonagenarians and those past one hundred who had traveled to Normandy for the eightieth anniversary of D-Day.

But unlike her grandmother, Marjorie wore the same style clothes as her daughter, was the same size, and religiously colored her hair a mahogany brown. People assumed she was ten years younger than she was, and she rarely corrected them. Her own mother, Alice, had also looked much younger, not allowing herself to go gray and soliciting and following Marjorie's fashion advice.

Not going gray, Marjorie was convinced, was the key. Some of her friends had opted for the easy way out during

COVID and now claimed they were delighted to be free of the burden of coloring their hair every month and even enjoyed it when people held doors open for them. But Marjorie was vain and enjoyed people thinking that she was younger than she was. She had no desire to be treated like a little old lady and could open doors for herself and others, if need be. Now that she was retired from her teaching job, she had a standing appointment every other Wednesday afternoon with her hairdresser of thirty years at Sequoia Salon.

When the salon first opened, it sucked business away from the old-fashioned smaller shops, then called beauty parlors. The beauty parlors usually consisted of the owner and three or four other hairdressers. They were dark and narrow and looked like they were stuck in the early sixties, with some of their customers still getting their hair set with rollers and sitting under the dryer. If you wanted a manicure, the same person who cut your hair would polish your nails.

But at Sequoia everyone was a specialist. There were those who shampooed your hair, then there were the hairdressers, the manicurists, waxing experts, makeup artists, colorists, and facialists. Not only was the new salon large, bright, modern, and stylish, but there were so many hairdressers that if you couldn't get an appointment with one, you could always get a replacement. The salon was even open on Sunday, so if you had a special occasion you could get your hair done the same day.

Thirty years ago, when she first started going there, the receptionists at the front desk were warm and friendly. Even though it was a very large shop, they made it their business to know every customer by name. Marjorie used to joke that it was like the popular TV show *Cheers* without the alcohol. In the back of the shop there were coffee, tea, and cookies, and often bagels and cream cheese from the bagel store in the same shopping center. It had such a friendly vibe. One customer used to bring in pizza on Friday afternoon and share it with her hairdresser and other customers and staff in nearby stations. Sometimes she even sneaked in a bottle of red wine.

In the salon, there was a little boutique that sold costume jewelry, knock-off purses, and other random items. People bought things they didn't need, but it was therapeutic somehow. Sequoia was definitely the place to go, and after a day at work, Marjorie enjoyed meeting friends and neighbors there.

Marjorie developed a relationship with her hairdresser, Teresa, whom most people called Terri. They confided in each other—Terri complaining about her husband and Marjorie unloading about whatever it was that bothered her that week: her boss, her mother-in-law, the parents of her students. It was the one time in the week when she felt completely relaxed because she trusted Terri implicitly. Besides, they didn't travel in the same circles, so who could Terri repeat Marjorie's stories to?

During COVID, Terri had even come to Marjorie's house to cut and color her hair in the backyard.

Once the pandemic ended, it took a few months for Marjorie to get her sea legs, but she was soon back to her routine of going to Sequoia. And she went back to getting her hair colored every five weeks or so. Terri had a formula for a rich mahogany color, which generated Marjorie many compliments. Terri was delighted when Marjorie recommended her to friends and former colleagues.

About a year after the world had moved on from COVID and people discarded their masks and started going to restaurants, the movies, weddings, and bar and bat mitzvah parties, Terri told Marjorie that the owners of Sequoia were planning to move the shop.

"The landlords have raised the rent astronomically, and the owners found a better location a couple of miles down the road. It's going to take months until renovations are completed on the new shop. And it's going to be spectacular."

Marjorie was not a person who was attached to places or things. She had moved from her home of more than thirty-five years to a gated community and never thought twice about the physical house she left behind. So the news was not of great import to her, except that the new Sequoia would be closer to her home, which was a plus.

When Marjorie went to the new shop for the first time, she noticed it was very bright and modern looking—everything was a blinding white, except for the black chairs at the individual stations. And there was loud, unfamiliar music blaring. Joan and Carol, the two longtime receptionists, were still there, thankfully. Gone were the coffee and snacks.

But Marjorie was there to see Terri and dismissed the changes. She noted, though, that all of the prices had been raised substantially and there was a big sign that if you paid by credit card, the cost was an additional 4.5 percent.

"Will there still be any special promotions?" Marjorie asked Joan.

"No." Joan rolled her eyes.

Marjorie had especially loved those special deals, sometimes forking over as much as $1,000 to get $300 in free services. But Terri later explained to her that the owners simply couldn't afford the promotions and the coffee and snacks because they had sunk so much into the new shop.

Soon, shockingly, Joan and Carol were gone, replaced by two ultra-skinny twentysomethings dressed in black. Marjorie noticed that Terri was also in black.

"Everyone who works here is now required to wear black," Terri told her.

As Marjorie got her hair washed by Louisa, who was in her sixties, she asked her, "What's with the whole staff in black?"

"It's part of the vibe," Louisa said. "They want to create a young vibe. The older customers aren't going to be around forever and they are trying to attract a younger clientele."

Well, thank you very much, Marjorie thought to herself as her heart sank. She knew full well that she was getting older, but who needed a reminder, especially here?

"What do you mean by *young*?" Marjorie asked.

"In their twenties," Louisa said.

"Really?"

Marjorie scanned the room and it looked to her like most of the women were in their fifties, sixties, and seventies. She spotted her friend Jan Rosenzweig, who was there with her mother, Helen.

Helen was a regular at Sequoia. She was there every Wednesday to get her hair and nails done. Marjorie went over to the station where Helen was having her hair styled; her daughter sat in the empty chair next to her.

"Hi, ladies," Marjorie said cheerfully. "And happy birthday, Helen!"

"Hi, Marjorie," Jan said. "Are you coming to my mother's birthday luncheon tomorrow?"

"Of course," Marjorie replied. "I wouldn't miss it for anything. When is your actual birthday, Helen?"

"It's today. I'm 103. Can you believe it?"

"Happy birthday," she said as she bent down to give Helen a kiss. "You don't look a day over eighty. You're gorgeous."

And Marjorie was telling the truth. She looked at this woman with a sparkling smile, dyed auburn hair, in full makeup and her nails polished in a bright red. She was bursting with self-worth and confidence.

"Thank you."

"How many women are coming?"

"Thirty," Jan said. "Our Hadassah chapter has been throwing a party for Mom ever since she turned ninety. And it gets bigger every year."

"That's wonderful. Can't wait. Let me ask you a question, Helen."

"Of course." Helen smiled.

"Are you comfortable in this new salon with the new look and feel? Louisa told me they're trying to cater to young people."

"You mean the bright lights? Better to see the job they're doing. I think if they want to stay in business, they have to cater to all of their customers, especially the regulars. How many young people can afford these prices? Right, Mitchell?" Helen said to the male hairdresser who was styling her hair.

"Of course, Helen. You know you're my favorite."

Helen beamed.

It occurred to Marjorie that this 103-year-old was adapting to change better than she was. This woman was a generation older and she wore her age gracefully. She clearly had all of her faculties, but most important, she was cheerful. She was not staying up at nights worrying about getting older. In fact, she relished the attention and respect she garnered.

"What's the secret to staying young?" Marjorie asked Helen.

"No one *stays* young, but you can have a positive attitude about getting older. Don't let others define you. Of course, nowadays I don't really have many contemporaries, but I love hanging around with younger people, especially my grandchildren and great-grandchildren. I read and play word games. I get my hair done every week. I put on makeup every day for myself, but also because I don't want to scare anyone. And, of course, I'm blessed with Jan, my wonderful daughter, who visits me every day in my apartment and takes me out."

"But we live in such an ageist society," Marjorie said.

"That's hardly news," Helen replied. "Look, I've known for at least forty years that our society equates youth with beauty. We live in such a shallow culture. Older women become invisible. Men no longer view you as a sexual being, but you get over that. And let me tell you a secret, it's actually a relief. You don't have to prove anything. I'm grateful for every day I live. Yes, it's hard to get in and out of cars, and I do have aches and pains, but so do people much younger. I have so much more confidence than I had when I was younger. I don't care what people think of me. And the best part of it is that most people are amazed that I still have all my faculties, and they seek out my opinion."

"When did you start telling people your age?"

"I have to confess I wasn't always so forthcoming. I used to like people to think I was younger. But now I'm proud of it. Actually, my husband outed me at his ninetieth birthday party, which unfortunately was his last. He announced that he had robbed the cradle when we got married, that I was five years younger than he was. So, I decided to own it, and I'm grateful for every year since."

"Wow," said Marjorie. "Just one last question. What do you think of the word *elderly*?"

"Do you have a better one?"

"I'm thinking about that one."

"Look at Chinese culture," said Helen. "Older people are venerated. They are seen as family and social treasures. They're considered to be wise, and their opinions are valued."

"I definitely think we need a new word," Marjorie replied. "Actually a new way of looking at aging."

"I wouldn't be that concerned about semantics, Marjorie. Just try to cultivate a positive attitude and be thankful for every day."

"Well, thanks for the therapy," Marjorie said. "I'll see you at the party tomorrow."

As she got into her car with ease, Marjorie thought about Helen. Was she just a congenitally positive and happy person, or could an attitude like hers be cultivated? She had to admit that she would like to bottle Helen's attitude, but was it too late for her? Or did she just overthink everything?

Marjorie knew she looked and felt good, but she could see that time was passing faster than ever. She could see it in the aging of her children and in the amazing growth and development of her grandchildren. How long could she remain active and relevant? She thought about all the time she had wasted worrying when she was younger. Yet, she had no desire to relive her youth.

Tomorrow, she would help to celebrate Helen, who gave no thought to how others viewed her. Marjorie wished she could be as comfortable as this 103-year-old woman was in her own skin. Perhaps just living, and not analyzing, was the secret.

Epilogue

Candles

One hundred and eight candles
For every year lived and
One for next year.
Hadassah members throw a birthday party
Every year
For their eldest member
Each year except for the pandemic
When it was on Zoom.
Smack in the middle of February,
The birthday honoree
Gets her hair done for the occasion
And holds court with her daughter's friends
Sharing the secrets of a long life,
As if there are any.
She loves parties,
But not this year,
Because she's slowing down a bit.

One hundred and three candles
That's the number
That would have been

Should have been
On my mother's birthday cake today.
But we lost her at eighty-five
And there was so much more
For her to see and enjoy
And love.
It's an age that seems not so old now.
When octogenarians are running countries
And making movies
And giving their opinions on cable TV.

One candle
There should have been one candle
On his birthday cake
White with blue icing and balloons
Surrounded by family and friends.
The sweet, smiling baby boy
Kidnapped on October 7.
The terrorists, who found the time
While they were raping and beheading
And slaughtering Jews
To snatch the innocent infant and his blameless brother
As their mystified mother held them close.

Only yahrzeit candles
No birthday cakes
For the one and a half million Jewish children
Murdered by the Nazis.
And for their parents and grandparents
And aunts and uncles and cousins
And the generations that will never be.

Shabbat candles
Every Friday before sundown
Before darkness descends
A time of tradition, petition, promise
An act of hope and faith

May our prayers be heard.

Glossary

afikomen: A piece broken from the middle of the three matzahs used by Jews at the Passover Seder service and set aside to be eaten at the end of the meal. It is traditionally hidden during the Seder to be searched for by the children present.

***aliyah*:** (Hebrew) Going up. It has a double meaning. It is the honor given to a worshiper of being called to say a blessing during the Torah reading. In addition, it means moving to Israel.

***Baruch HaShem*:** (Hebrew) Blessed be the name of the Lord.

***bashert*:** (Yiddish) Destiny. Commonly used to refer to finding one's soulmate.

bima: The podium or platform in a synagogue.

***boker tov*:** (Hebrew) Good morning.

***bubby*:** (Yiddish) Grandmother.

cantor: A member of the clergy and accomplished singer who leads a Jewish congregation in worship services.

***chai*:** (Hebrew) Life.

chuppah: Marriage canopy.

Dachau: The first concentration camp established in Germany in 1933 shortly after Hitler became chancellor. It became the model and training camp for all other concentration camps. It was notorious for the

German doctors and scientists who used inmates as involuntary guinea pigs for medical experiments, such as infecting prisoners with malaria, treating them with various drugs with unknown effects, and testing the effects of going without food or water.

davening: Praying.

Dayenu: Traditional Passover hymn, literally meaning "It would have been enough."

dreidel: A small four-sided spinning top with a Hebrew letter on each side, used in a children's game traditionally played at the Jewish festival of Hanukkah.

gelt: Coins.

haftarah: A selection from one of the biblical books of the Prophets, which is read during Sabbath services after the Torah reading.

Haggadah: The book containing the text recited at the Seder on the first two nights of Passover, including a narrative of the Exodus.

hamantaschen: Three-sided pastry with fruit filling, traditionally eaten by Jews during Purim.

***hamsa*:** (Hebrew and Arabic) An ancient Middle Eastern amulet symbolizing the hand of God. In all faiths it is a protective sign believed to bring its owner happiness, protection, health, and good fortune.

Hanukkah: Eight-day Jewish holiday commemorating the rededication of the Temple of Jerusalem after its defilement by Antiochus of Syria.

hora: Traditional Israeli circle dance.

***kiddush*:** (Hebrew) Sanctification. It is a blessing recited over wine or grape juice to sanctify the Shabbat and Jewish holidays. It also refers to refreshments served after Sabbath or festival services.

***kippah*:** (Hebrew) Skullcap, yarmulke.
"Kol Chasson v'Kol Kallah": Traditional Hebrew wedding song in honor of the bride and groom.
kosher: The Jewish dietary laws.
Kristallnacht: The wave of violent anti-Jewish pogroms, which took place throughout Germany and Austria on November 9 and 10, 1938. Windows of synagogues and Jewish homes were shattered and Jewish-owned businesses were plundered and destroyed.
kugel: A sweet or savory pudding of noodles or potatoes.
kvell: Burst with pride.
***lashon hara*:** (Hebrew) Gossip.
latkes: Potato pancakes.
***machar*:** (Yiddish) Important, influential person.
matzah: Unleavened bread eaten during Passover.
mazel tov: A Hebrew phrase meaning "good luck!"
Mensa: A nonprofit organization and the world's oldest and largest high-IQ society.
***mieskeit*:** (Yiddish) Ugly person.
minyan: Quorum of a group of at least ten Jews required for a prayer service.
mitzvah: Commandment; in common language, often used to denote a good deed.
***nachas*:** (Yiddish) Pride.
Passover: The major Jewish spring festival that commemorates the liberation of the Israelites from Egyptian slavery, lasting eight days.
***peyos*:** (Hebrew) Sidelocks.
Purim: Festive Jewish holiday celebrating the Jews' escape from a plot to harm them.
Seder: The ritual meal and home service Jews observe on the first two nights of Passover. The word *Seder*

comes from the Hebrew word for "order," referring to the instructions, readings, and songs detailed in the Haggadah.

***shanda*:** (Yiddish) Shame.

Shehecheyanu: Prayer of thanksgiving.

***shidduchim*:** (Hebrew) Jewish arranged marriages.

shiva: Seven-day mourning period.

***shlep*:** (Yiddish) To pull or carry something with difficulty.

shul: Synagogue.

Torah: The Five Books of Moses (also known as the Pentateuch): Genesis, Exodus, Leviticus, Numbers, and Deuteronomy. These five books together form the first and most sacred third of the Jewish Bible.

***vort*:** (Yiddish) Celebration of an engagement.

WAC: Women's Army Corps, women's branch of the US Army.

yahrzeit: The anniversary of the death of a parent or close relative.

yarmulke: Skullcap, kippah.

Book Club Discussion Questions

1. The first story, "Remember to Eat," discusses Marjorie's labor and delivery and her husband's reaction to those events. Do you think his behavior was typical of his generation, and, in your opinion, are today's young men different?

2. In Part 2 of "Remember to Eat," Marjorie's toddler sons wander off while she's in a department store. Have you ever had a similar experience? If so, how did you feel? What did you think of Marjorie's reaction?

3. In "Mother-in-Law," what do you think about the relationship between Marjorie and her daughter-in-law, Cara? Do you think their interaction will change after the wedding? If so, how? If not, why not? Is there something inherently difficult in the relationship between a mother and her son's wife?

4. In "Fighting Hitler: Alice's War," do you think Alice's relationship with Gisela, the German Jewish teenage girl who came to live with her family, influenced Alice's desire to enlist in the military? What did you think of

Alice's decision to join the army in World War II?

5. In "The Nazi House," how does the specter of WWII and the Holocaust play a role—particularly, how does it influence rumors about Lilli and her family's disappearance from their home in Queens?

6. In "After the War," Alice and Connie compare their busy and meaningful lives in the army to the post-war years, where they are baking for the school bake sale. The two women eventually decide to go back to work, although few women work outside the home in that era. Why do you think they make this choice?

7. Do you think Alice and Connie would have had a different trajectory to their careers if they were alive now?

8. In "Nobody's Child," what did you think about Marjorie's behavior after the death of her mother? What did you make of her dalliance with Jonah? What did it mean, if anything?

9. Marjorie's bond with her daughter, Deborah, is highlighted throughout the book. Do you think Marjorie has the same expectations about her relationship with her sons that she has of her daughter?

10. In "Cherished Daughter," how is Marjorie's outlook about Deborah unrealistic once her daughter has a family of her own?

11. Do you think mothers have different expectations for their relationship with married sons than married daughters? If so, explain.

Acknowledgments

From the time I was five years old, I remember my mother sitting at the kitchen table at her manual typewriter. She was writing a memoir of her experience as a staff sergeant in WWII in the Women's Army Corps. When I heard the clicking of the keys, I knew then that writing was something I wanted to do. I told my mother I, too, wanted to write a book—about my experience in kindergarten! I had barely learned how to write the alphabet, but instead of pointing that out to me, she gave me a couple of sheets of paper. Obviously, I didn't have that much to say and couldn't fill the pages. But I still somehow understood the great power of the written word.

My mother's memoir was never published, but much later—when she was eighty—she captured her memories, and the history of our family, in a lengthy tome. She said she wrote it just for my brother Arthur and me, and for our children, her grandchildren.

The "Alice" stories in *Remember to Eat* are inspired by my mother's childhood, youth, and army life. While I fictionalized them, they were motivated by her memoir—as well as the many stories and anecdotes she told me throughout her life. I don't know whether she'd approve of how I've reimagined them, but then again, she always praised whatever I did! So, I'm going to think she would have loved the book. She has been gone for many years, but she is always with me—especially when I'm writing.

My mother was an amazing human being, and a loving and supportive mom, wife, and daughter. She matter-of-factly told me how she joined the army in World War II right after she graduated from NYU in 1943, motivated by her patriotism and desire to do her part in fighting the Nazi menace. She had a post office romance with my father, Herbert Fischman, of blessed memory, who served with General Patton's Army in the Battle of the Bulge. They were married for sixty years until his death. The characters of Alice's parents are based on my maternal grandparents, Mary and Harry Trachtenberg, whose love and devotion brightened my childhood.

I also want to acknowledge my friend and former colleague, MaryPat Grafstein. Besides being a wonderful educator and generous friend, she shared her mother's WWII experiences with me. Her mother, Mary Elizabeth Conway Morris, nicknamed Connie, was an army nurse who has been designated an official Liberator of the Dachau Concentration Camp; her army hospital unit was the first in the camp. She also served in hospitals on the front line during battles and campaigns throughout Algeria, French Morocco, Tunisia, Italy, and more. She is an official member of the Survivors of the Shoah Visual History and her memories are housed in the Library of Congress. MaryPat gave me both her mother's written materials and recordings, which helped enormously in crafting my character Connie Murphy.

I am deeply grateful to Brooke Warner and Shannon Green for helping me bring this book of short stories to life. And I am thankful for Crystal Patriarche and her amazing team at Booksparks, including Tabitha Bailey and Rylee Warner for promoting and publicizing it.

I appreciate all those who have helped me to polish my work and get it out in the world: Mikayla Butcher, Cait Levin, Krissa Lagos, and Rachel Sherman. And I am especially indebted to the awesome Kylie Ora Lobell for her tireless efforts on my behalf.

Thank you to Pam Stack for giving me a platform on the Authors on the Air Global Radio Network and embracing the notion that it was a good idea to have a podcast featuring Jewish books and authors. I am so appreciative of Kerry Schaefer for all of her assistance in bringing the *People of the Book* podcast to the airwaves.

Thank you to all of the fantastic members—both authors and readers—of my Facebook group, Jews Love To Read! Together, we have provided strength, encouragement, and insight to one another. Thank you also to the amazing Renee Weingarten, who supports authors like me through her fantastic Facebook group, Renee's Reading Group. Also, I am so appreciative of Linda Levack Zagon of Linda's Book Obsession for championing my work and being so kind and helpful. Special thanks to Briann Shear for connecting authors with the group Hadassah Book Clubs. As a lifetime member of Hadassah, it is always a joy to meet (physically or virtually) with fellow Hadassah members. Thank you to Zibby Owens for her efforts in advancing Jewish authors and books. I also want to thank Sylvia Jacobs (Books and More 1818) for her support. And a shout-out to Elissa Wald for creating the Never Alone Book Club and creating opportunities for Jewish authors.

I have a wonderful network of people who have been more than caring, generous, and helpful in cheerleading my books and providing opportunities for me to share my work: Ellen Zuckerman, Linda Landow, Jane Pomerantz, Karen Spitalnik,

Eve Feldman, Ellen Grebstein, Phyllis and Curt Lader, Rabbi Howard Buechler and Laura Buechler, Myrna Kopel Green, Shelly and Harvey Lefkowitz, Harriet and Michael Goldstein, Chevi Kail, Ann Grafstein, Fran Cooper, Phyllis Frank, Ellen and Peter Albert, Randi Brenowitz, Bayla Lovens, Sarrae Crane, Rabbi Jonathan Waxman, Jennifer Feingold, Audrey Atlas, Shelly Gross, Susan and Stewart Kampel, Susi Wood, Wende Jager-Hyman, Silvia Kogan, Ira Faber, Karyn Likerman, Lisa Travis, Batsheva Slavin, Beth Mann, Marsha Schiffman, Rabbi Avraham Bronstein, Rabbi Marc Schneier, Julie Zuckerman, Laurie Birzon, Stuart Tauber, Cheryl Caiazza, Barbara Burstein, Heidi Levine-Sorkin, Robin Feins, Rabbi Alysa Mendelson Graf, Joani Madarash, Karen Savader, Sharon Solomon, Joan Turman, Deborah Green, Thane Rosenbaum, Francine Klagsbrun, Linda Ettinger Lieberman, Linda Lidor, Linda Scholnick, Alice Fossner, Amy Newman Connolley, Rabbi Steven Moss, Leigh Evans, Michelle Harrison Gross, Carol Levy, Melanie Glass, Penina Bredoff, Roberta Slatkin, Belle Rosenbloom, Ronni Reed, Merri Ukraincik, and Michael Hammerman.

Thank you to my sister authors Valerie Taylor, Jackie Friedland, Jacquie Herz, Marilyn Simon Rothstein, Esther Amini, Gila Green, Deborah Kalb, Michelle Cameron, Roni Robbins, Linda Rosen, and Jean Meltzer for their friendship and support.

I also want to acknowledge Gladys Meresman, the mother of Ann Grafstein. Until her death at the age of 109, she continued to be a role model for succeeding generations with her positive attitude, and she was an inspiration for me as I wrote this book.

Many thanks to my brother, Arthur Fischman, and his wife, Janet Margolies, for always lending an ear and a hand. Thank you to my nieces, Anna Fischman and Molly Fischman, for keeping my mother's memory alive.

I want to express gratitude to my husband, Stewart, for his enduring encouragement and for always commenting on what I write, making suggestions to improve it, and being a good sport. Thanks also to my children and grandchildren for lighting up my life in too many ways to enumerate.

About the Author

photo credit: Diana Berrent Photography

Meryl Ain is a writer, author, podcaster, and career educator. She is the author of two award-winning post-Holocaust novels, *The Takeaway Men* (2020) and *Shadows We Carry* (2023). Her articles and essays have appeared in numerous publications, and she is the coauthor of a nonfiction book, *The Living Memories Project: Legacies That Last*. She is the host of the podcast *People of the Book* and the founder of the Facebook group Jews Love to Read! She holds a BA from Queens College; an MA from Teachers College, Columbia University; and a doctorate in education from Hofstra University. She and her husband, Stewart, a journalist, live in New York and spend the winters in Boca Raton, FL. They have three sons, three daughters-in-law, and six grandchildren.

Looking for your next great read?

We can help!

Visit www.gosparkpress.com/next-read
or scan the QR code below for a list
of our recommended titles.

SparkPress is an independent boutique publisher delivering high-quality, entertaining, and engaging content that enhances readers' lives, with a special focus on commercial and genre fiction.